May you learn that it is okay to be selfish with yourself

PLAYLIST

1. Kehlani—Can I
2. Justin Bieber—Company
3. Wale, SZA—The Need To Know
4. ZEINA—Nasty
5. Ambre, Jvck James—I'm Baby
6. Quin, 6lack—Mushroom Chocolate
7. Lucky Daye—Guess
8. Babyface, Ari Lennox—Liquor
9. Beyonce—SUMMER RENAISSANCE
10. Victoria Monet, Bryson Tiller—We Might Be Falling In Love
11. Khalid—Better
12. Alicia Keys—Un-Thinkable
13. Alex Isley, Jack Dine—Such A Thing
14. 6lack & J. Cole—Pretty Little Fears
15. Paolo Nutini—Better Man
16. Coco Jones—ICU

ONLY
FOR THE
WEEK

NATASHA BISHOP

ONLY
FOR THE
WEEK

PROLOGUE

Janelle

1m

Arnold Hightower

Hey

1m

Arnold Hightower

Sorry to hit you up like this but I thought you should hear it from me - I'm proposing to Amerie

1m

Arnold Hightower

This weekend

YOU ARE INVITED
TO THE WEDDING OF

Amerie Cross

&

Arnold Hightower

AUG

THURSDAY **17** AT 1 PM

2023

RIVIERA MAYA RESORT
TULUM, MEXICO

Reception to follow

PART ONE

THE CALM

CHAPTER ONE

Janelle
Months Later

"**A**ND YOU'RE SURE YOU HAVE EVERYTHING YOU NEED? PASSPORT? Phone charger? Deodorant?"

I roll my eyes, thankful my mom can't see me through the phone, as I shove another book into my suitcase. Without fail, my mom always calls me to run through a checklist whenever I go on a trip. I could remind her that at my big age of thirty I'm capable of packing my own bag, but what would be the point? I'm going to get the list regardless, it can either be with attitude or not.

I choose not.

"Yeah, Ma, I got everything. Double and triple checked."

"Okay, what time you headed to the airport?"

"Evie should be here in about twenty minutes."

"Good, good. And you're sure you're okay to go on this trip, sweetie? I swear, I don't know what your sister was thinking, tacking on an extra week when this is already uncomfortable for you."

There it is. The reason why I can't wait for this wedding to be over is not the fact that the bride is my sister, and the groom is my ex-boyfriend. It's the fact that everyone keeps bringing it up with pitying glances like I'm some sad sack hung up on the guy.

Fun fact: I was over Arnold Hightower before we even broke up.

We just weren't a match. It took a year of us being together for me to finally see that, but once I did, he agreed, and we went our separate ways. No fanfare. No hard feelings. No nothing.

Yes, when he popped back into my life six months later on the arm of my older sister, I was surprised. Who the fuck wouldn't be? But that's all it was, shock. I knew they were a much better fit than Arnold and I ever were the minute I saw them together. Hell, I was the one who comforted Ri when she started panicking that they were moving too fast due to Arnold proposing after three months. I was the one who convinced her not to break things off, and yet somewhere along the way, everyone deluded themselves into thinking that I'm some heartbroken woman scorned that's barely holding onto my sanity.

The shit is ridiculous.

"Mom, I'm good. An extra week in Tulum is exactly what I need right now." Beautiful weather, beaches, and a private pool? I will be living my best life for the next week until the wedding madness begins.

"You're so brave, baby."

Lawd. I need to get off this call.

"Yeah, thanks, Ma. Let me go so I'm ready for Evie."

She lets me hang up without too much fuss and I release the deepest of breaths. The trip hasn't even started yet and I'm already exhausted.

From my bedroom upstairs, I hear my front door open and Evie's loud ass walk through.

"What's up, biiiitch?" she yells.

I walk down the stairs to find one of my best friends, Evie, dressed in jean shorts and a white t-shirt that does nothing to hide her bright pink bra underneath, helping herself to a sparkling water out of my fridge.

"Why is it that you're so damn loud every time you step into my shit?"

Whereas Amerie went to fashion school in Georgia and our other best friend, Dani, moved to New York to pursue modeling, Evie and I stayed together. Both of us went to Howard University for undergrad and we both came back home to Baltimore after so I could go to medical school at Johns Hopkins and so she could get her graphic design career started. We stopped being roommates during my last year of residency, but we've always had keys to each other's places and she always lets herself in my place in the loudest of ways.

She shakes her head at me. "You may have forgotten 'The Honey Incident', but I haven't."

"What the fuck is the...oh my God."

"God is who I was praying would burn that shit from my retinas and memory but no such luck."

"I told you Chris was really into food play. If you didn't want to see him licking honey off every crevice of my body you should've called first."

She sticks her finger in her mouth and pretends to gag. "What is the point of calling first when I have a key?"

"Ask them supposedly burned retinas of yours."

She laughs around her sip of water. "That's okay, I like my method of announcing my presence, it gives you the chance to put all the condiments away before I step fully inside."

"First the fuck of all, I'm not even with Honey Boy anymore so stop it. Second of all, is honey even technically a condiment?"

"It's too early for trivia, Nelly."

My nose wrinkles as I look at the clock on my oven. "It's ten a.m."

"Too early," she waves me off. "Get your shit so we're not late for our flight to the wedding of the century."

I chuckle at the tight smile on Evie's face because I know she wants this wedding to be over as much as I do.

I love my sister, I truly do. But our relationship has been strained to put it lightly and her being a bridezilla while planning her wedding hasn't helped. I'm her Maid of Honor while Evie and Dani are bridesmaids and she's been relentless with her demands.

What's the difference between eggshell white and raindrop white? I unfortunately know now. Even getting her to settle on the location of the wedding was a headache. She knew she wanted a destination wedding, but she couldn't decide where. Arnold was no help, so Evie and I had to take charge and decide for her. Did we pick Tulum because we wanted to go there? Yes. But we also knew both she and Arnold would love it once they came out of their weird wedding tyrant haze.

When Amerie suggested the wedding party go to Tulum the week before the wedding festivities to just relax, I was excited. After dealing with the Prima Donna for months on end, we've all earned time to decompress before all fifty of Amerie and Arnold's guests descend upon us.

3

We pull up to the airport a little bit before eleven a.m. Evie has a love/hate relationship with time. Time loves her but she shows it no respect. She'll probably be late to her own funeral, but one thing she does not play about is flights. Despite being a bonafide jetsetter, she's deathly afraid of flying so she always gets to the airport two hours early in order to get her mind right and prepare to pop a Xanax.

Arnold's groomsmen, Micah and Christian, show up not too long after us. Micah stands at about six-foot-seven with rich dark brown skin, shoulder length locs, and a chiseled jawline. Normally, his style is more artsy so it surprises me to see him in a black sweatsuit right now, but damn does he look good in it. It angers me a little bit that I met and started dating Arnold before meeting the fine ass men he surrounds himself with; sure, Arnold's fine too, but physical attraction without compatibility never goes far.

Christian is the definition of a pretty boy, and he leans into it. He has deep sepia skin, light brown eyes, and his hair and facial hair are never out of place. Even his eyebrows are styled to perfection. He's about six-foot-two but his confidence is that of a seven-foot-tall giant. Where Micah is sexy but he stays under the radar, Christian advertises that he knows he looks good. The man has never met a pair of grey sweatpants he didn't like and today is no different.

Micah pushes his locs off his face as he walks over and bends to give Evie and I a kiss on the cheek. "Ladies, how you doing?"

"Great, Micah. How are you? Still fine as fuck, I see." Evie makes no attempt to hide her head-to-toe perusal of Micah. He smirks at her assessment, but doesn't return the perusal.

Christian clears his throat before bending down to give me a kiss on the cheek then standing to face Evie. "Evelyn," he offers.

"Christian." She shoots back.

"Still saying whatever the fucks pops into your head, huh?"

"Sure am. Still trying to stick your community dick in every pussy you see, huh?"

He chuckles while rubbing his hand across his jaw. "You're still mad about that? This is starting to sound less like women solidarity and more like jealousy."

"The only thing I'm jealous of is your ability to become an even bigger asshole the more you talk. You know you were foul to fuck my nail tech while dating my waxer. And what's worse is they both banned me from their shops just because of my association with you. Had me walking around looking like a wildebeest for weeks."

Micah's eyes bounce back and forth between the two, curiously.

Christian takes the seat next to Evie. His voice drops to a sensual timbre when he says, "Well your nails look fine to me. I'd be happy to inspect your wax job too, if you want."

Evie adjusts her position in her chair and for a moment I think I'm going to have to slap her for being affected by those fuckboy words but then she turns to face Christian head on, pressing her freshly done pink ombre coffin style nails into his forearm. "Christian, I say this with all sincerity, I would rather have my pussy waxed with sandpaper, than ever let you near it."

His eyes blaze with a fire so intense it threatens to suck all the air out of the terminal.

"Y'all done with your foreplay? I'm hungry," Micah asks.

"Not foreplay, just giving your boy the dose of humility he's sorely missing in his life. But yes, I'm done. Can you grab me something while you're gone, Micah?" She bats her eyelashes at him.

Micah gets her order and I tack mine on too before he and Christian leave without another word.

While they're gone, Evie fires up her laptop to do some last minute work for her clients and I stare out at the tarmac.

I can't remember the last time I took a consecutive two week vacation. The other doctors at the practice make time for vacations, but I never do. I have what I consider a healthy work life balance. Sure, I work twelve hour days with minimum breaks and when I'm not working at the obstetrics practice, I'm working on the plans for the birthing center I want to open, but I make sure to go to brunch with my girls once a month and I answer everyone's texts and phone calls in a reasonable amount of time. To me, that's work life balance. Going two weeks without seeing a single patient, though? Unheard of for me. There's a first time for everything, though.

"Look who we found," Christian's voice booms through the terminal.

Evie sucks her teeth but turns with me to check out our newest arrivals.

Dani, Amerie, and Arnold all walk behind Christian, but I can't focus on them because walking up beside Micah is a face that throws me completely off my game.

Of all of Arnold's friends, I've spent the least amount of time with his best man, Rome. When I was with Arnold, we were always two passing ships in the night. I'd get to Arnold's place only to find out he had just left. He'd bail on game nights at the last minute. When we did see each other, it seemed like he was always rushing off to do something else.

In the back of my mind, I always felt a tinge of annoyance at his absence because it felt purposeful. What the hell did I do to him to make him avoid me? I never let my thoughts linger on him for too long, though; scared of what feelings they might bring up.

Then he moved to California for six months for work. By the time he got back, Arnold and I were out and Arnold and Amerie were in. The first time we were in close proximity was when we were forced to work together to plan the engagement party. I barely escaped that party with my panties intact.

Rome Martin is gorgeous. He's not as tall as Micah but he has a good nine inches on me at six-foot-five. His taut muscles broadcast his familiarity with the gym. His ochre skin never has a blemish on it. His eyes are hypnotizing. They're the color of midnight, tempting you to plunge into the pits of darkness with them. The line-up on his taper fade is crisp. His beard is close cut but long enough at the chin for me to grab and hold on to. *Nope.* Cancel out those thoughts. It can't happen.

Just as Rome's eyes meet mine, I turn away. I don't have time for those deep onyx pools of trouble. Though looking at him and thinking of my earlier conversation with Evie about Chris reminds me of the Costco sized box of condoms Evie shoved in my suitcase against my will. If I come home with a few of those missing, I'll consider this trip a success.

My gaze turns to Amerie, donning white lounge pants and a white tank top. When she told me she planned to go all Lisa Raye and wear white every day of the trip leading up to the wedding, I thought she was joking. I should've known she wasn't. She flips her three-strand twist out behind her shoulder before strutting over to me like she's entering a boardroom.

Dani, who's wearing an orange jumpsuit that makes the mahogany of her skin pop, runs and jumps into my arms for a hug.

Arnold looks put together as always. As the son of an NFL legend and a sports agent himself, he's constantly "on", so I'm not surprised to see him dressed in tan linen pants with a white casual shirt like we're about to head to dinner on the beach right now instead of sitting on a four hour flight.

He hugs Evie but when it's time to greet me, he gives me one of those awkward side hugs. It takes everything in me not to snap at him that his dick was not good enough for him to treat me with kid gloves. I've had good dick, fantastic dick, and life changing dick. Arnold's wasn't bad by any means, but it definitely wasn't life changing. It wasn't even fantastic. It was just good; and I am not going to spend a year crying over simply good dick. I'm damn sure not going to let him make me feel like I am. The only thing stopping me from putting him in his place is knowing that anything I say will get back to my mom and further the narrative she's built in her mind. I'd rather just get the wedding over with and then fall back.

I catch Rome's eye again and my eyes widen slightly when he heads in my direction. His thick legs carry him over to me in no time at all. "You know, Ri was just telling me that you said your speech was gonna make her cry. I hope you're not trying to outdo me." Damn, that voice of his. Deep and sultry, a panty-melting melody.

This is the most off-guard I've seen him around me, and I can't help but want to pull more out of him. "I wasn't aware it was a competition, Rome."

He licks his lips; the movement sends a chill straight to my core. "Isn't it, though?"

"It's absolutely not. But if it were, I'd suggest you give your speech first. Because you'll be booed off the stage if you have to follow me."

"Is that right?"

"Very much so."

In the back of my mind, I'm aware that our eye contact is going on for too long but I'm also aware that he doesn't seem keen on breaking the connection either. So, I let it linger.

And linger.

Until finally, someone clears their throat forcing us to take a step back. "I guess we'll see," he utters before breezing past me to say his hello to Evie.

A retort stands at the tip of my tongue, but my mouth dries up at the feel of his hand on my skin as he walks by. I wonder if he felt the same shock I did.

I'm grateful for the reprieve when Amerie links her arm through mine. "I'm so nervous."

"For what? The flight?"

"No. I don't know. Just the whole trip, I guess. The wedding is really here. It feels like just yesterday we were in the beginning of the planning stage."

Not for me, considering I was ready to snap her neck back then. It took a lot of wine to get through that initial planning phase. "It's gonna be beautiful. Everything is gonna go just right."

"You promise?"

"Have I ever steered you wrong?" She shakes her head. "Exactly. So you just need to kick your feet up and relax this week. Let the stress come when Mom and Dad get here on Sunday."

"Oof, big facts. Mom called me this morning to ask me if you remembered your passport." *Of course she did.* "How would I know that? Anyway, you're right. I just need to get my ass into first class and get a drink to kick this whole trip off."

My arm slips from hers. "First class?"

She turns to me in confusion, which only serves to bring the blood boiling in my body closer to the surface. "Yeah? We're all in first class, aren't we?" She looks around the row of seats we've claimed for ourselves for confirmation and everyone but Evie and I nod their heads.

"Evie and I didn't book first class because when I asked you if you wanted to, you said you didn't see a point in paying the extra fee."

Dani chimes in. "Oh, she told me that too, but I said why start a luxury trip in Coach? So everyone switched up."

"Not you caping for her just because she's the bride," Evie chastises.

Dani snorts, sticking her tongue out at Evie. "I only cape for myself, thank you. I'm just saying it's my fault she switched it up last minute, so I'm sorry."

I internally roll my eyes. Amerie and I met Evie and Dani in high school and have been friends ever since. We even went so far as to call ourselves DEJA vu for the first letter of our names. I love these women. I would do anything for them. But, fuck, do I want to slap some fucking sense into both Dani and Amerie right now.

Even if what Dani said were true, it would still be Ri's fault considering she knows she had a conversation with me where she told me not to book first class and then did not follow up with me to let me know she changed her mind.

I look to Evie, whose lips are pressed together and eyes are hard.

"We could've just flown private like I suggested," Christian quips.

"It's the fact that you actually think you're helpful for me," Evie says, shooing him away with her hands.

"Well, why don't we go over to the desk and see if they can upgrade your tickets? My treat." Amerie shrugs.

Now, I'm just insulted. I can pay for my own first class ticket, she should know that's not the damn point.

Stop what you're doing and count to ten. It's her wedding vacation, you can't go off on her.

I take a deep breath, trying to dispel my anger.

Ten.

Nine.

Eight.

Seven.

Six.

Five.

Four.

Three.

Two.

One.

Fuck that, I'm still pissed.

"I'm good. I'll stay where I am."

Her shoulders sag. "Nelly, it's not a big deal. I can just…"

I interrupt her. "You're right. It's not. That's why I'm not gonna bother upgrading."

I hear a faint "oop" come from Dani's direction and then nothing. The silence permeating our little corner of the terminal is deafening. Regret digs its teeth into my skin at the despondent look on Ri's face. She just told me she was nervous and I never want to add stress to her plate, especially when this should be the happiest time of her life, but I'm so exhausted. I make a promise to myself to put my perfect Maid of Honor hat back on once we get off the plane and without another word, I turn away from her and sit down to pull out my phone.

> Me: Sorry. If you want to upgrade, don't let me stop you

I purposefully messaged Evie on Facebook so that she could answer from her laptop and not make it obvious we're talking.

> Evie: *eye roll emoji* on today's episode of Things I Already Know.

> Me: Lmao fuck you

> Evie: I'm riding with you heaux

> Evie: And before you ask if I'm sure… shut up. Before I really let you be dusty musty crusty by yourself

> Me: So unserious. Goodbye

> Evie: Wait hold up…you think I can get Micah to slide me some dick this trip?

> Evie: Scale of 1-10

> Me: *inserts gif of 'I said good day' from Willy Wonka*

> Evie: Now you're already a sad and lonely bitch over Arnold's ass let's not add hater to that list. It's not cute

> Evie: *insert gif of Jackee laughing*

A derisive snort slips past my lips. Evie catches my eye to send a subtle smirk and wink my way, so I reach up to scratch my nose with my middle finger.

An overwhelming sense of being watched falls over me and without looking I somehow know I'm going to find mesmerizing onyx irises when I lift my head.

Sure enough, there he is sitting a mere row over, manspreading because it's impossible for the chair to hold all of him. Fuck, the man has tree trunks for thighs.

His eyes remain fixated on me, not in judgment and not even in lust, just unbridled curiosity.

What do you want from me, Rome?

Almost as if he can hear the thought cross my mind, he looks away, turning his attention to his phone.

This is about to be the longest two weeks of my life.

A little while later, we've finally boarded the plane. Evie popped her Xanax twenty minutes ago, so I know I only have her company for maybe another ten before she's out. Probably less, because she's already starting to lean her head against the window. She squeezes my hand just before her eyes flutter closed. Definitely less than ten minutes.

"This seat taken?"

My head whips around to face the voice that I'm sure I couldn't have heard.

Nope, I heard it alright. What the hell is he doing here?

"You lost, Rome? First class is that way," I point in the direction of the front of the plane.

He must be more conscious of the other people boarding the plane than I am because he quickly breaks eye contact to lift his carryon into the overhead bin. The move causes his hoodie to lift just enough to catch a glimpse of the cut of his abs. I move to the middle seat, so he won't have to climb over me to sit down. I can't be held responsible for my actions if his dick gets too close to my face.

He folds himself into the aisle seat beside me with a shrug. "A woman was having an issue so I offered her my seat."

"An issue? What kind of issue?"

"The kind where she discovers her boyfriend is cheating on her as they're boarding this plane together and is seconds away from having a nervous breakdown."

My jaw drops. "Oh shit."

"Yeah."

I tear my eyes away from his to scour the plane. "Where is the guy? I'ma boo his ass."

I lift up from my seat but his hand locks onto the crook of my arm as he wheezes out a laugh. "Ayo, you can't do that!"

"Why not?" I shrug. "He shouldn't have cheated on my girl."

His brows jump to his hairline. "You don't even know the woman."

"I know nobody deserves to get cheated on, so if he can embarrass her like that then he can get embarrassed too."

He studies me closely, nodding his head slowly, processing each of my words carefully. His assessment makes the back of my neck heat, but I resist the urge to pull the collar of my shirt away from it.

"Gray hat. Pink-ish shirt."

I search all over until I find him a few rows behind us.

He takes his hat off to run his hand through the maple brown layered fringe mop on his head. Even sitting down, I can tell he's tall but also on the lanky side. The color of his shirt drowns out his alabaster skin. He's sitting next to a gorgeous Black woman with amber skin and a blonde short twist bob. My jaw goes slack when I see him do a sniff test on his shirt and then turn a charming smile on the woman. What the fuck?

Rome whispers to me that the ex-girlfriend just stuck her head out from first class to scowl at the man. I lean over him to get a glimpse of her, but Rome's heady scent fills my nostrils and blinds me to everything else around me. He smells like wood directly after a rainstorm. It's a comforting smell, one that makes me want to curl up in his arms for a nap.

I give up on trying to see the ex, needing some distance from Rome, so I turn my focus back to the cheater behind us. He's chatting up "Ms. Short Twist Bob" without a care in the world.

Fuck this man. He's walking around looking like James' peach but has the nerve to play in another woman's face immediately after being exposed as a cheater.

If there's one thing men are never short on, it's audacity.

I hold up my phone and snap a picture of the man.

"I just know you're up to no good right now. What you got going on?" Rome asks.

"Just working a little magic on Canva."

He leans over my shoulder to look at my screen, invading my senses with that damn scent again. I retype the same line three times before I'm able to shake off his hypnosis.

He cups his fist around his mouth and lets out a howl of a laugh. "Ayo, you're really sending that out?"

"Hunnid percent," I deadpan as I hit the button that would airdrop the image I created to all Apple users on the plane.

Rome pulls out his phone when it pings with the notification to give the image another onceover. He shakes his head in amusement and turns that gorgeous grin on me. "You're a savage."

The flyer I sent out is a wanted poster with the picture I took of "Mystery Guy" on the forefront and a transparent photo behind him of a man in a lab coat holding a long cucumber in one hand and a small pickle in the other. The caption reads 'Have you seen this man? Owner of a small dirty dick incapable of keeping it in his pants. Last seen in any and everyone's dms. If found, please return to the streets.'

"And don't you forget it."

I look around the plane at numerous passengers receiving and laughing at the post. I can tell "Ms. Short Twist Bob" got it because she looks from her phone to "Mystery Guy" with disgust and twists her body away from him. A boisterous laugh drifts from the front of the plane and a smile crosses my face at the hope that "Ms. Dodged A Bullet" received my gift.

The icing on the cake is when "Mystery Guy" himself sees it. His head flies up to search the plane but when he realizes he doesn't have an ally because most people are either laughing at him or looking at him with shame, he shrinks back into his seat and pulls his hat back over his hair.

Damn, that felt good.

The flight attendants announce the plane's approaching departure and run through the safety precautions before heading to their takeoff seats.

A peaceful quiet falls over Rome and I, with Evie's soft snores serving as our backup music.

"Is she good? She's slump over there," Rome points to Evie.

"Oh yeah, she's good. The power of Xanax."

"Ah, not a fan of planes then. My dad is the same way. He refuses to go on any vacation where he can't drive, take a bus, or train."

"I guess it's safe to say he won't be coming to this then."

"Absolutely not. He told Arnold not to even waste an invite on him. Him and my mom are gonna stay home and watch my nephew when my brother gets here next week so it worked out."

"So, how's your mom feel about your dad's international travel ban?"

He chuckles. "She couldn't care less. She travels with her friends and sisters and leaves his ass at home whenever the mood strikes. She told him if she fucks around and finds an international side piece, he'll have no one to blame but himself."

"Your mom sounds like my kind of woman."

"I think so too. She would've loved how you obliterated ol' boy."

I put my hand to my chest then throw my hand out. "Why, thank you. That was light work."

"I could tell. Remind me not to get on your bad side."

"What would be the fun in that?" I tilt my head to the side in question and he playfully rolls his eyes.

The plane starts its descent down the runway, calling my gaze to the window. I watch with rapt attention as the wheels lift off the ground and the runway becomes smaller and smaller until there's nothing in sight but clouds.

When I peek back over at Rome, he's watching me intently. Was he speaking? "Sorry, I love to watch planes take off."

"It's no problem. What do you love about it?"

No one's ever asked me that before. I feel like there are two kinds of people: window seat people and aisle seat people. Let's face it, no one willingly chooses the middle seat, but no one really asks why each group prefers one over the other. It just is what it is.

"There's a freedom in literally watching your problems disappear beneath you. In giving someone else the control to carry you away from reality for a while. Does that sound stupid?" I hold onto the tethers of my control so vehemently that it's liberating when I have no choice but to give it up. The very thing that terrifies Evie about flying exhilarates me.

He shakes his head earnestly. "Not at all. It actually makes perfect sense." A sense of appreciation washes over me at his affirmation. "So, why aren't you sitting in the window seat?"

"I always let Evie sit in the window seat, so her head doesn't bobble around when she passes out."

I expect Rome to laugh with me at my comment, but he doesn't. He leans back in his seat, seemingly mulling over my words; picking them apart and chewing each one piece by piece and the look he gives me when he refocuses tells me he doesn't like their taste.

"Do you make it a habit to sacrifice things that make you happy for others' comfort?"

I bristle at that. His words slice through my defenses faster than I can build them back up, leaving me speechless. Trying to buy myself some time to come up with anything to say, I force out a cough. I can't decide if I'm more offended because he doesn't know me or because he sees too much.

"It's not like that. It's just not a big deal because I can still see out the window. You've never compromised for someone you care about?"

"Of course. I'm sorry, I didn't mean to come off like I was judging you. I just think sometimes we lose ourselves in our compromises and forget that 'no' is a full sentence." He clears his throat.

The rest of the plane falls away as silence stews within our bubble, simmering into acceptance and understanding.

"Got it. So, when the flight attendant comes around for drink orders, I'll get both the tequila and white wine instead of compromising down to one," I quip, needing some levity to break up the intensity of this interaction.

He seems to appreciate the moment coming to an end and laughs along with me. We switch to much lighter topics and before I know it, the pilot chimes in over the speaker to announce our arrival in Cancun.

"Damn, that plane ride flew by," he says as he stretches his arms out. "Are you gonna watch the plane land?"

My lips split into a wide grin. "I sure am. There's a method to my madness. I always watch the takeoff from home and the landing at my destination, but not vice versa."

"Because the landing at your destination means you've reached your safe haven away from whatever plagues you at home. Takeoff from your vacation spot symbolizes the end of peace and landing at home means watching your problems take center stage again."

Well shit.

"Exactly. You get it."

"I try. Here we go." I turn to face the window, watching the beauty of

Mexico grace us but my body is buzzing with an awareness of Rome's proximity over my shoulder.

Once the wheels hit the runway, my head bounces back slamming into the brick wall known as Rome's chest. He reaches his hand up to smooth the dull ache at the back of my neck. Why does his touch feel so right?

"You good?" His voice is a faint whisper, but I feel it in my belly.

"All good." Relief floods me when he doesn't stop rubbing my neck.

Evie stirs beside me, shattering whatever fucking trance we fell into. She blinks her eyes open, assessing her surroundings.

"Shit," she whispers to herself. Her brows furrow when she turns and sees Rome, much further away from me than he was mere moments ago. "When did you get here, Rome?"

We laugh at her confusion and recap the story of the cheater, drawing a cackle out of her that garners the attention of the two rows in front of us.

Getting off the plane is uneventful. We're able to grab our bags in no time at all and as we wait for Ri and Arnold to grab the rental cars that will take us from Cancun to Tulum, Rome and I keep circling each other. Dani talks my ear off about how Christian acted up in first class, but my focus keeps drifting back to Rome and when I catch sight of him his eyes seem to always be on me.

"Okay, cars secured. Let's ride! Girls with me," Ri orders, walking off without waiting for confirmation from anyone.

I take one last look at Rome before turning to follow.

CHAPTER TWO

Rome

MICAH AND CHRISTIAN'S VOICES DRIFT IN THE VERY BACK OF MY consciousness but I can't make out a word they're saying. I can barely recall a word they said the entire trek to Arnold and Amerie's room. The hotel we're staying in, The Dahlia Resort, is absolutely insane. When we arrived, we were partnered with a personal concierge, named Javier, who will be available to help us if we need it and can recommend sites and activities. Apart from Arnold and Amerie, we each have our own suites, with backyards that are covered in beautiful greenery and have a private pool. The view is breathtaking, but I can think of one better and my focus has been firmly planted on her since the moment I saw her today.

Janelle is the epitome of beauty. From her gentle eyes to her full lips against her umber skin down to her curvaceous body that has haunted my every dream since the day I met her. Every time I've seen her prior to this trip, she's worn her hair in its natural curls, but today her hair falls down her back in box braids with loose curly pieces making it appear fuller and wilder.

She piqued my interest immediately. She commanded the room with her warm smile alone. The problem was that I met her as she was being introduced to everyone as Arnold's girlfriend. I'd love to say that I'm such an amazing friend that my instant attraction to her died precisely when Arnold uttered the word girlfriend, but it didn't. My eyes never strayed far from her for the rest of the night. The sway of her hips demanded more of my attention than I cared to admit. And when I spoke to her? I was lost in the soft, melodic tone of her voice and by the end of the night, it was my favorite song. We talked about everything under the sun. She was attentive and inquisitive about my career, and she was passionate about her own career as an ob-gyn and how much she loves helping women. We even talked about her dream to open a birthing center that focused on the reproductive health of all women of color. Something in Janelle's soul spoke to me that night. It unlocked a part of me I didn't even know existed, but fuck if I wasn't thankful to experience it.

Still, I would never do my boy like that so I decided to do the only thing I could. I kept my distance. I'd leave Arnold's house when I knew she was headed over. I stopped going to game nights when she was there because the one time I did allow myself to go, she and I were paired against each other and her fierce competitive spirit had me ready to risk it all.

When my video game publishing company, Downhill Studios, had an opportunity to team up with a company in California to produce a new crossover game, I jumped at the chance. Twenty six hundred miles was exactly what I needed to get Janelle out of my mind. I blocked all of Arnold's posts on Instagram so I wouldn't have to see them together and I went about my business.

I was grateful that I was still in California when the two broke up. I thought I was over it but her being newly single only put her in the forefront of my mind again. I needed more time and space to put her behind me because the one thing I'd never done and never planned to do was make a move on someone one of my boys cared about.

That all changed when Arnold started dating Janelle's sister and suddenly I wished I was back home. I was blown away. I've never known Arnold to do something shady like that. Everything in me wanted to reach out to Janelle to see if she was okay, but I knew it wasn't my place. Instead, I reached out to Arnold, but he was very vague on the details.

I'd spent a fragment of time with this woman. It should've been a blip on my radar, and yet she's occupied every corner of my mind.

"Right, Romey Rome?" Christian slaps the back of his hand against my shoulder.

"Huh?"

He shakes his head, laughing. "You ain't hear a word I said, did you?"

"I told you he was over there daydreaming," Micah adds.

"What you dreaming about? Gameplay design?" Christian chuckles to himself and I just flip him off.

"Nah, I'm good. I'm tired as hell, though." We did just get off a four hour flight and come straight here so I'm hoping that's a good enough excuse.

"Well, you better wake yo ass up. We have dinner in an hour. Ri just texted that she's on her way to the room to change so I'll catch up with y'all." Arnold daps each of us up, effectively dismissing us from his room.

A phone call with my brother and my nephew causes me to be the last one to show up to dinner. There's a private dinner set up for us along the beach. The bright white flowers adorning the table illuminate the area against the dark backdrop of the sky, giving an almost glowing effect. This should be a simple dinner for just us, but it looks like a premiere event. I expect no less, though, considering all the painstaking details that went into the wedding planning.

The table seating; however, throws me off guard. We're sitting at a large rectangular table, four seats on each side and two at the heads, but since there are only eight of us, I have three seats to choose from. The other head of the table, the seat directly next to Micah or the seat directly next to Janelle. It strikes me as odd that Arnold would sit at the head of the table with Amerie on the side of him instead of letting her be the head or leaving those seats empty and sitting beside her. If it were me, I'd never dare to occupy the throne while my wife-to-be sits in the number two position. She'd sit on the throne while I guard her back. I shake the thought away. Not my business.

"Sorry I'm late, y'all," I announce.

"It's all love, man. We just ordered our drinks so you're good," Micah gestures to the open chairs.

I'm not about to sit at the head of the table opposite Arnold, so it's either next to Micah or next to Janelle. I decide that sitting next to Janelle is the best option. If I'm sitting right beside her then my eyes won't wander to her too often.

Big mistake. Once I sit down, I'm immediately enveloped in the scent of her perfume. It's something citrusy and floral. It perfectly embodies her; sweet and sensual. If that wasn't bad enough, I get the full effect of her outfit and I'm undone. She has on a brown long sleeve wrap crop top with a matching maxi skirt. Her abdomen is covered with three lines of waist beads in white, gold, and brown; each begging me to remove them with my teeth and her skirt has a slit that exposes her entire succulent thigh. I'm fucked.

She adjusts slightly in her seat when I sit down but her eyes are friendly when she turns to me. "I thought the guests of honor were supposed to be the fashionably late ones," she says, poking fun at me.

"Well, sometimes you just have to make a grand entrance. You know a thing or two about that, I'm sure."

Her smile deepens. "At least you know."

"You look beautiful." Maybe I should've kept that thought to myself, but all common sense goes out the window with her.

Her smile falters for a moment but then she picks her head up and beams. "Thank you. You look nice yourself." She looks me up and down in appreciation, laughing when I flex my arms.

"Pst, Rome," I look up to find the source of the faint whisper is Evelyn leaning behind Janelle's chair.

"What's up, Ms. Eve?"

"When you order your drink, you should get a Bay Breeze. Just saying." Her voice is hushed but her words are slow.

Janelle rolls her eyes, but I can see the twinkle of laughter in her eyes. "She's been telling all the guys about this drink since we sat down. Safe to say she's a little obsessed."

"It's my new favorite."

"Mhm, and how many of your favorites have you had tonight?" I ask.

"I'm about to get my fourth."

"You know, Evelyn," Christian interrupts. "I didn't take you for a sloppy drunk. I'm so surprised at your behavior." He puts his hand on his chest in mock offense. Micah groans and Dani rolls her eyes.

Evelyn cuts her eyes to Christian. I didn't even think she was capable of moving that quickly in her state, but her movements are swift. "Do you ever get tired of hearing yourself talk? Because let me tell you, it's day one and I'm already exhausted of it."

This is Eve and Christian's standard state of being around each other. Normally, when two grown ass adults go at each other this hard I would say they need to fuck and get it over with, but I'm pretty sure Eve actually wants to murder Christian, so maybe not.

"Why would I get tired of hearing myself talk? This voice is like butter, baby. Why you think they put me on the radio?"

Christian is the host of one of Baltimore's most popular radio shows, Hot Takes. He likes to say he melts the panties off every Baltimore shorty from seven to nine p.m. every night.

"Because they didn't wanna show your face," she deadpans.

He scoffs. "Now you know that's cap."

"I need another drink. I had a nice buzz going on and you killed that shit."

"You could get a nice buzz off me instead," he licks his lips.

"Oh, brother! This guy stinks!" Dani shouts.

"Sandpaper, Christian. Sandpaper." Eve takes the last gulp of her drink, setting the glass on the table with disgust.

"Is y'all done or is you finished?" Arnold asks.

"Is your friend done shooting above his level or nah?" Eve scoffs.

While they continue to go back and forth with barbs and Amerie attempts and fails to referee, I turn my attention back to Janelle.

"So what are you drinking?"

She eyes me over the rim of her glass, licking her lips to wipe the drink residue away when she's done. One subtle movement from her has my dick ready to jump out of my pants.

"A Mezcalita," she pauses. "You want to try it?" She holds her glass out to me, mischief shines in the chocolate brown of her irises.

I take the glass from her outstretched hand, ignoring the sensation that creeps through my body at the contact from our fingers.

The minute my lips touch her glass, her eyes blaze and her breath escapes in a sharp hiss. I register the taste of the mezcal and pineapple juice sliding down my throat. I even register the coarse texture of the tajin rim against my tongue. The drink is fine, but I can't stop imagining how it would taste on Janelle's lips.

She clears her throat. "Do you, um, do you like it?"

"It's not my favorite drink, but it's good."

She tilts her head to the side, taking me in. "What's your favorite drink?"

I take a moment to study her, gliding my gaze down her form, lingering a second too long on those God damn waist beads, and then back to her face. "I haven't had it yet."

Her jaw drops but she doesn't have a chance to say anything before the waiter enters our peripheral. She leans down to ask, "Bienvenido. Can I get you a drink?"

Everything in me wants to keep the connection Janelle and I have right now. Pull her down the rabbit hole of lust with me, but I know I've said too much already, so I turn my attention to the waiter. "I'll have what she's having," I say.

She turns to Janelle, then eyes the drink in my hand, and nods. "Not a problem."

She asks the table if we're ready to order appetizers and Arnold takes over, ordering for everyone. I couldn't care less what we eat but when I turn back to Janelle, she's deep in conversation with Eve. *Shit.*

Once the appetizers are ordered, Janelle and I fall back into easy conversation but the moment is no longer charged like it was earlier. I don't know what made me push things like that when I said I wasn't going to explore the emotions she has me feeling but fuck I can't resist. Resisting Janelle is like resisting the urge to breathe. It tears you apart from the inside out until there's only fragments of you left.

Quite frankly, I'm tired of trying.

"Hey, Nelly, did you remember to bring the picture of Pops with you to add to my bouquet?"

The past two hours at dinner have been full of this. Every time Janelle gets comfortable or gets involved in a conversation not centered around the wedding, Amerie tosses her a random wedding related question to reel her back in.

Janelle clenches her first under the table, then smooths her hand over her knee. "Yeah, Ri. Remember I showed you earlier?"

"Oh, right. Okay, thanks." Amerie turns her attention back to Arnold, giving him a megawatt smile and quick peck on the lips. "Oh, wait but did you bring the pink ribbon I wanted to tie around my bouquet for Wheezie since she can't come because of her treatments?"

I catch Janelle grip both her knees tightly before speaking through clenched teeth. "We never talked about a pink ribbon on your bouquet, Ri."

The entire table stops in their tracks.

"Yes, we did. I remember telling you I wanted to do that. Why wouldn't I want to honor Wheezie?"

Wheezie is their aunt who is currently battling cancer. From what I hear from Arnold, her chemo is going well, but she's unable to travel at the moment. If I remember correctly, though, it's Janelle who's extremely close to Wheezie whereas Amerie checks in out of obligation.

Janelle swallows deeply and I wonder what thoughts she just choked back. I wonder if anyone else notices the storm brewing in her eyes. I catch glimpses of resentment, rage, melancholy, and defeat all before she blinks them away into a state of neutrality.

How often does she mask her true feelings for those around her?

She clears her throat as she rubs her fists up and down her thighs. "You're right. I'm sorry. I'm sure I can find some pink ribbon here though."

Amerie's eyes sink to the table.

"I'll help you look," Eve offers.

"Yeah, it's not a problem. I can get Javier to point us in the right direction. I've already bonded with him," Dani laughs.

Micah's eyes cut to hers, but she doesn't seem to notice before he hones back in on his drink.

Janelle's focus remains perfectly planted on Amerie, who is looking everywhere but back at her.

Christian and Micah both look at me, but I'm too busy looking at Arnold wondering why he's not saying anything or at least making a move to comfort his fiancé.

Something tells me that what Janelle needs at this moment is a chance to breathe, and giving Janelle what she needs is somehow becoming a necessity for me.

I grab my glass and tap it as I stand. "Before we wrap up for the night, I just wanna say a quick word. Amerie, there's still time to get you out of here if you wanna run." Everyone at the table laughs, including Janelle, which is all I wanted. "Nah, but really, congratulations you two. You have built something special here and I'm excited to celebrate with you. Thank you for letting me be a part of this."

"Wouldn't have it any other way, man," Arnold raises his glass to me.

"To longevity and prosperity," I say, quoting Arnold's motto to him and everyone else.

"Cheers," everyone says in unison.

Finally, dinner is over and everyone decides to call it a night, feeling the effects of the long day.

"Walk with me to our rooms?" I hear Eve ask Janelle.

She smiles in return, but it doesn't reach her eyes. "I'm actually gonna go for a walk on the beach first. I'll see you in the morning?"

"You sure you're good?"

"Yes," she drags out the word. "I just need to feel some sand in my toes."

Eve rolls her eyes. "Such a hippie. Aight girl, see you in the morning. Text me when you get back to your room though so I know I don't have to come fuck someone up."

"Yes ma'am." They hug and I watch as Eve heads in the direction of her room with everyone else while Janelle heads in the opposite direction.

Go to your room.

Do not follow this woman like some kind of creep. Go to your room.

My feet feel heavy, probably because I already know which direction I want to go. I'm just waiting for my head to get the message across that it's a bad idea.

The message never comes.

I don't know when it happened but somehow my body got my heart and my mind to be on the same page with it.

When I catch up to Janelle, she looks like a dream. I take a moment to mentally capture the image of her so I can keep it if she decides to turn me away.

"Hey," I say, quietly hoping not to startle her.

It seems to work because she turns to me in a lackadaisical spin. "Hey, Rome. You not tired?"

"Nah, not yet. I wanted to get some fresh air before heading back."

"Me too."

"Do you mind if I walk with you?" I ask even though both of our feet have already started carrying us further down the beach.

"I don't mind," she whispers.

The stress on her face during dinner keeps playing in my mind. The clear hostility between her and her sister plagues my every thought. I heard from Christian that there were rumors that Janelle was hung up on Arnold and so things were awkward but that never struck me as true, and not just because I don't want it to be. Even during dinner tonight, there was no tension between Janelle and Arnold. She barely paid him any attention, in fact. The heat was strictly between Janelle and her sister.

"I'm gonna ask a question and I'm sure it's a question you hate and I hate that I'm asking but I'm going to do it anyway. Feel free to tell me to fuck off."

She chuckles. "Well after that build up, I can't say I'm excited but go ahead."

"Are you okay?"

She skids to a halt, turning to face me. I wait for the animosity in her gaze, but it doesn't come. Instead, her eyes are soft and inviting, reeling me in so fast I can't seem to stop it. "Honestly, I'm surprised it took you this long to ask. Even Christian's self-absorbed ass asked me when everything first happened. I was beginning to think you didn't give a fuck about me." She shifts from one leg to the other and I reach out to grab her hand.

"Janelle, I..."

She puts her hand up to stop me short. "I'm just fucking with you. I do hate that question but I know you meant well so it's fine. You weren't around a lot when Arnold and I were together, so you didn't see but we just weren't right for each other. I mean, he was basically just the homie that I happened to be exclusively fucking. There was never that spark, that something. You know?" Of course, I know. Because I think she and I have it. "But him and Amerie? They just fit. So, I couldn't be happier for them. Really. I just don't know how I became the spinster in this story. Shit, if anything I'm the God damn Fairy Godmother." She looks down at her feet but I grasp her chin and force her eyes back to mine. "My parents," she stops and laughs humorlessly. "Not my parents, my mom. My dad knows me better than that but I think he's just trying to survive his wife. Anyway, my mom thinks that because I haven't dated anyone seriously since that I'm obviously not over him and am just putting on a brave face. I guess I'm just wondering when my value became tied to a man in her eyes. Can't I have the freedom to just…be? To love myself enough to be comfortable in my own company? If you want to get real about it, I've been happier being alone and keeping things casual than I ever was with Arnold. I'm sorry, I know that's your boy but I'm just tired of having all of these emotions placed on me that I don't feel."

I can't lie, hearing her say that she never felt a deep connection with Arnold unleashes something in me. The will to keep it at bay dwindles with every passing moment.

"You have this energy about you that puts people on high alert. When you walk in a room, everyone knows they're in the presence of greatness and for some, that can be overwhelming."

"Does it overwhelm you?" She asks, tilting her head further.

"Not at all. I'm just happy to exist in your orbit."

A small gasp slips through her lips, almost imperceptible but I catch it. I lock it in as my new favorite sound that I vow to hear from her in every way possible.

I don't know who moves first, but our lips connect. Her lips are soft and warm, timid but all consuming. I grab her waist and pull her flush against me, eliciting a sweet moan from her. Her hands lift and I think she's about to grab my shirt and pull me in but she pushes against my chest instead.

"I am so sorry. I shouldn't have done that," Her voice comes out in heavy pants. "I…oh fuck. I shouldn't have done that."

I grab her hand and stop her rant before she can hurt my pride. "I like how you just took all the credit like I didn't kiss you too."

"Okay, but…"

I cut her off. "But nothing. You telling me you regret it? That you don't want more?"

Her jaw drops but her lidded eyes tell me exactly what I need to know. "I dated your best friend."

"And yet, he's marrying your sister."

Her lips twist into a frown as she squeezes my hand tighter. "So what? I should just be petty?"

"It's not about being petty. It's not about them at all. What is it that you want? I get the feeling you don't do enough of that."

"Enough of what?"

"Enough of what you want."

"Bold of you to assume that you have anything to do with what I want."

"I'm not trying to be bold; I'm just hoping you're feeling even a tenth of what I am."

She tilts her head, squinting her eyes. "What is it that you're feeling, Rome?"

As I contemplate my next words, I keep asking myself is this worth it? Is doing this with Janelle, even if it'll only be one night, worth the potential fallout with one of my best friends if he finds out?

There should be some sort of doubt in my head, right? Some feeling that I need to take a step back and rethink things? I consider myself to be a good man so there should be some hesitation here. Shouldn't there?

There isn't. The only answer on my mind is yes. She's worth it all.

"I feel like I need you. I need my lips on yours and my hands on your body. I feel like I need to make you feel good right now or I just might explode."

I can feel the moment she makes her decision.

Her body relaxes against me and her arms drape over my neck. She searches for something in my eyes and the moment she finds it, she exhales deeply. "Fuck it," she says as she pulls my face down to hers.

CHAPTER THREE

Janelle

"**O**UCH," I CRY OUT AS MY HEAD HITS THE BACK OF MY DOOR. Rome and I have been a mess of limbs and tongue since the second kiss, bumping into so many surfaces as he carried me back to my room. I knew he looked like he could handle me but having him carry me the not-so-short distance from the beach to my room without breaking a sweat or our kiss only made me more wanton for him.

"Shit, I'm sorry."

"No. Don't stop. Don't you dare stop," I say, sealing our lips back together. I never want this to end. I've never been a person who needs to do a lot of kissing during sex, but kissing Rome is different. It's a sexual experience all on its own and I just want to drown in him.

What I don't tell him is that I'm afraid if he stops, the doubts will creep in and be the reason I drown instead.

There shouldn't be anything wrong with Rome and I having sex. We're two consenting adults. The problem is, if my family finds out about this, it won't be that simple in their minds. They'll see it as a whole vengeance plan to get back at the people who "fucked me over". What a stupid fucking thought.

"Hey," Rome's voice is so commanding it stops me in my tracks. "Whatever you're thinking about, leave it be. It's just you and me right now. Stay with me."

Why did I hear forever after that statement? Now, *that* is a stupid fucking thought.

Be in the moment, Janelle.

I need this release. I want it and more importantly, I fucking deserve it.

With that, I give him a determined nod and grab the hem of his shirt. He lifts his chest away from me to help me get the shirt over his head. It's then that I realize he doesn't have his hands on me at all. I'm locked against my doorway with nothing but my legs wrapped around his waist and yet I've never felt more secure. Good God, I am a lucky woman tonight.

His eyes darken as I lift my hands up to undo the knot in my top, revealing that one I wasn't wearing a bra tonight and two my nipples are already hard. He wastes no time bending so that he can pull my left nipple into his mouth, grazing it with his teeth. I hiss and my back flies off the door when he blows on it to soothe the bite. "Oh shit."

Releasing the left one with a pop I catch a smirk on his face as he turns his attention to the right nipple, showing it the same exact love and care.

He secures his arms under my ass and then backs up slowly until he reaches the end of the bed and right when I think he's going to lower us down, he turns and drops me on my back. I don't even get a second to catch my bearings before he scoops me and pushes me up toward the headboard.

"Everything about you is so intoxicating," he mumbles as he pulls my skirt and thong off my legs, leaving me in nothing but my waist beads. I reach for the chain to disconnect them, but his hand shoots out to stop me. "Aht aht, those stay."

My brow raises. "You want me to leave the beads on?"

"Yes. They've been driving me crazy all night. Taunting me with how they caress your skin." I love accessories. My belly button is pierced and I have multiple piercings in my ears. Waist beads, thigh chains, and headpieces are never far from my wardrobe. I make a mental note to display them more during this trip. *The fuck am I saying?* This is one night. One night only.

"Taunting you, huh? I like that."

"You like driving me crazy?" His eyes never leave mine as he rubs my foot, placing a kiss on the side that's as warm as he has me feeling. "You like making me desperate for you?" He kisses my ankle next. "Making me fantasize about how you sound moaning my name?" Next, my calf. "How you taste on my tongue?" I squirm when he kisses my inner thigh. Fuck, I need his mouth on me right now. He's barely touched me and I'm already on the brink of ruin.

"I do. But, if you were really desperate for me, you'd already know how I sound moaning your name," I tease.

He chuckles and I feel his breath against my sex, so close to where I need him and yet miles away. "Nah I'm taking my time with you, J." He's never called me J before. No one has, but I like the way it so easily rolled off his tongue. It makes me feel…things I shouldn't be feeling. Not for Rome.

Chills roll up every surface of my body when his tongue breaches my center. I come alive under his attention, hungry for everything he has to give me and even more after that.

He flicks and twirls his tongue and nose all through my pussy, glazing over my clit but never staying long enough. *Motherfucker is toying with me.* I run my hands over his hair, down his face and over to the spots behind his ears, massaging them firmly. Right as I'm about to push his head further down, he latches onto my clit and sucks the soul right out of my body.

My hands fall from his face and fist the sheets tightly, trying to keep a firm grasp on reality but it's too late; I'm already lost in whatever universe he transported me to. His fingers join his tongue, pumping in and out of me until all I can hear is the slickness of my wetness and my cries of pleasure.

"Oh my fucking God, just like that," I cry out. He hums his acknowledgement, sending a buzzing sensation over my pussy. Rome doesn't need direction; he knows exactly what he's doing to my body, but I'm doing whatever I can to keep my soul here on this plane of existence. I can't afford to miss a moment of this. I wrap my legs around his shoulders and press the heel of my feet on his back. He rises to the challenge and adds another finger to his delicious torture and sucks my clit even harder. This man is trying to kill me.

Though he doesn't complain, I realize I'm crushing his head between my thighs, so I drop them back down to the bed, not wanting to squeeze him to death before I get my nut.

My vision starts to blur with every pass of his tongue and I feel my body tightening. "I'm gonna come." The words are a tick above a whisper but the moment I say them, he stops. *What the fuck?*

"Not without saying my name, J." I want to be mad, but fuck if he doesn't look like my wildest fantasy right now. If I thought his eyes were trouble before, they're downright criminal when he's ravenous with my arousal dripping down his chin.

It takes an exorbitant amount of energy I don't have to lean forward so I'm closer to his face, and I know I'm going to regret the words I'm about to say but I can't stop myself. "Make me."

I know I fucked up the minute the devilish smirk crosses his lips. "Bet." He dives back in and in no time at all I'm right back to where I was before he cut me off. This is some damn sorcery. I've never had my body used so perfectly before and I haven't even seen his dick yet.

My legs start to shake beyond my control and my back practically levitates off the bed. "Fuck, Rome!" I scream, using the last bit of my energy to give him what he wanted. I feel the dam break and him lap at the juices like he can't get enough. He doesn't let up, though, sucking and fucking me into complete oblivion. "Rome, please," I moan.

He takes one final swipe to my pussy before kissing my inner thigh and sitting back on his haunches. "I was right," he says, proudly.

"About what?"

"You are my favorite drink."

My pussy throbs at his words. She's already grown attached to that tongue and that's not good. It's a problem for tomorrow's Janelle, though. Tonight's Janelle plans to drain Rome dry and let him do the same to me.

"What do I taste like?"

He pulls his pants down in one swift motion revealing his beautifully carved dick. He is literal perfection. His dick should be the mold for dildos everywhere. Ignoring my lustful stare, he crawls over my sprawled out legs, hovering over my lips. "Sin. Paradise. Everything."

"Show me." His lips come down to mine. How is it that every kiss with him is different? The one on the beach was sweet. It was tender and unassuming but passionate at the same time. The one against the door was hungry, messy, and wild. It made my heart beat so hard, I could feel it in my toes.

This kiss? It's possessive and consuming, threatening to swallow me whole and spit me out a completely new person. We've already set the perfect rhythm with each other as if we've been doing this for years and not minutes. Or has it been hours? I have no idea. This kiss digs itself deep within my bones and plants its roots in my bloodstream. The taste of myself coating his tongue floating between us only adds more fuel to my fire. He's right. This is pure sin and I love every second of it.

I wrap my arms around the back of his neck and pull him down so there's no barrier between us. His dick presses into my stomach causing me to shift in hopes of feeling that friction somewhere else.

He laughs when I hook my leg over his and use that leverage to flip us so that he's on his back. "You strong as fuck, girl."

I giggle. Fucking giggle. Who even am I? I may be a thick girl, but Rome easily has at least seventy to a hundred pounds on me. We both know the only reason I was able to flip him is because he wanted me to. "That's right. So you better give me the dick I deserve so I don't have to show you my strength in other ways."

"You really up there threatening to beat my ass if I don't deliver good dick."

"Are you gonna let me down?" I drill my eyes into his and he meets my intensity, though I can feel the humor radiating from him.

"No ma'am," he licks his lips as he says the words.

"Then you don't have anything to worry about." Without breaking eye contact, I reach over to the resort nightstand and grab a condom from the drawer. Looks like I'm going to make a dent in this Costco box after all. Ripping the condom open with my teeth, I lean down to wrap it around him with my mouth. It brings me joy to hear the rough exhale from him as I wrap my lips around him. He's lucky I can't go another second without him inside me or I would use every trick in my arsenal to drive him to the edge the way he did for me. There's still time for that, though, because I plan to make the most out of tonight. I rise onto my tippy toes to let his dick stand at attention beneath me, and then ever so slowly, I take him in.

"Ah, fuck," he grunts. "Keep going, take all of me."

I revel in the feel of him stretching me and when our hips connect I take a moment to appreciate the full weight of him inside me. I can feel him in my stomach.

"I'm so proud of you, gorgeous." He leans up to give me a quick kiss and I hate the way I preen under his attention. He's getting under my skin too quickly. He moves his lips to the shell of my ear and whispers, "Now, I need you to move for me."

Ask and you shall receive. I slowly lift my body so that I'm only sitting on the tip, settling forward so my breasts are in his face and then I slam back down and rotate my hips. His eyes roll in the back of his head on my second descent. "Shit," he drags out the word. "You feel fucking amazing."

Up and down. Up and down. There are no words exchanged, only gracious moans and contented hums. His hands caress every inch of my skin. His touch is so gentle until I bite his lower lip. He stops his exploration and plants his hands against the dimples in my hips. I know then that my time of being in control is over, but I don't mind. I want him to possess me. He thrusts his hips up to meet me, setting us on a new pace that is so wildly tantalizing I can barely breathe. That same feeling of dizziness takes over and all I can do is hold on and hope I survive the landing.

My toes curl so hard with my release that I'm afraid I'll get a full-on cramp. My legs are still shaking when he flips me onto my back and enters me again. He lifts the leg that was cramping the hardest over his shoulder and kisses it. It's hard to reconcile the sweetness of that action with the relentless way he's fucking me.

"You with me, J?"

"Yessss," I cry out. I clench around him and I know I got him by the grunt he lets out and the way he hangs his head.

"Nah, I'm not tapping out. Not til you give me another one."

The challenge in his eyes and the way he firmly presses his hand against my fupa lets me know he's dead ass serious. The pressure of his hand intensifies his stroke, making me clutch the sheets with barely there control.

"I...I ca..."

"Don't fix your lips to tell me you can't, J. This pussy is magical and I need to feel that power again, okay? I need to feel her milk me again. I need to hear her scream for me. You got me, baby?"

His words hit me right in the chest, strengthening my resolve. I've never felt such a strong desire to please someone before. I'll give him everything.

"I got you."

And I do. I rotate my hips in time with his and when that dizziness takes over again, I fall into it. I clench my walls around him, screaming out in ecstasy.

"Ah, fuck, J. Just like that. This shit is too good." His jaw clamps shut, and his thighs tighten as he calls my name with reverence while joining me over the edge.

After taking a minute to collect ourselves, he pulls out of me and my pussy twitches at the loss of connection. He falls to the side of me and pulls my body into his, kissing the top of my head. It's scary how comfortable I feel in his arms. My mind is telling me I should detangle my limbs from his and walk him out before this goes any further, but my mind is also tired as hell from the thorough fucking whereas my pussy is revitalized and begging for more. I can feel my heart trying to enter the conversation, but I don't have time for that bitch, so I tune her right out.

"Talk to me, J. What's on your mind?" Rome asks, staring at me intently.

I lift my hand to his face, taking in all his features up close. My thumb circles the line of his jaw just above where his beard starts. So smooth.

"You."

He smirks, his cheek curving perfectly under my hand. "What do I have to do to stay on your mind?"

You've already done it.

I bite my tongue to keep from saying just that. "You're a smart man. I'm sure you'll figure it out."

He sits up, leaving my hand to fall to the middle of his chest, before hopping from the bed. He darts to the bathroom and for a second the fear that he might deny me and leave creeps to the surface, but before it can fully form, he comes back out sans condom and cups his hands under my ass to pull me to the edge of the bed.

"Trust me, J. I'm nowhere near done with you." Any words I could've thought to say die in my throat the minute he picks me up as if I weigh nothing and carries me to the shower.

"Good morning, sunshine. How'd you sleep?" His voice is a sweet caress against the shell of my ear. I don't open my eyes but a smile spreads across my face.

"Sleep? What's that?" I question. I don't know what time it is, but I know it can't have been that long since we finally came up for air and closed our eyes. I don't even remember feeling Rome's body leave mine. My body must've realized if she kept listening to my pussy she was going to die, so she shut down on my behalf. Apparently, Rome had a little more energy though because there's no stickiness between my legs. He must've cleaned me up.

My head feels lighter, so I reach my hand up to find my silk bonnet covering my braids. I was not wearing this during our last round. He found my bonnet and wrapped my hair? Nevermind, there's definitely a stickiness between my legs now.

The deep timbre of his laugh heightens my arousal and I hope he can feel the heat radiating off me as he rubs my thigh under the covers. "Hey, I tried to let you sleep. You weren't having it."

Damn right I wasn't. I wasn't going to be satisfied until I drained us both completely dry.

"You complaining?"

My eyes flutter open hoping to catch his reaction to my teasing. I'm rewarded with his brilliant smile, every exquisitely white tooth on full display just for me.

"Not at all. Last night and this morning was perfect."

"It was."

Needing a reprieve from his menacing eyes, I turn on my side to grab my phone off the nightstand. It's plugged up to the charger, too. Damn, he really took care of everything.

I laugh when I reread all the texts from Evie last night. I managed to remember to answer her at some point between rounds to keep her from coming to my door. I don't know what I would've done if she came to my room and found Rome there. I know she wouldn't have snitched. Hell, she probably would've had a field day with it, but there's something inside of me that wants to keep him to myself.

> Evie: I know your ass ain't still on that beach!

> Evie: Where you at?

> Evie: Either you are the unluckiest bitch in the world and got kidnapped on your first day of vacation or you went to sleep without texting me first. Which one is it?

> Evie: My bed is very comfortable so you better be kidnapped heaux. On my way

> Me: Lmao my bad I dozed. Stay in bed and I'll do the same

> Evie: What did my college boyfriend used to call me?

> Me: Girl what?

> Evie: Making sure it's really you and not your kidnapper

> Me: Lol omg

> Evie: Omg these nuts answer the question

Me: Sigh

Me: Trey used to call you Creamsicle

Evie: Okay now delete that message so no one ever sees that cringe ass nickname and don't make me hunt your ass down again. Good night

Me: Ma'am yes ma'am. Good night

I turn my attention back to Rome, whose eyes are now closed again but his hand is still rubbing circles on my thigh.

"Thank you for taking care of me last night. And this morning."

One of his eyes pop open at my statement and I point to my bonnet and my phone on the charger.

He seems to wrestle with his response before an easy smile settles on his face. "I got you, J."

My throat constricts at that. It's time to go. My phone says it's nine a.m. and I know it won't be long before the girls come looking for me. Even knowing that, I make no moves to leave Rome's warm embrace.

"I know we're hitting the spa today. What are y'all doing?" Since I'm clearly not strong enough to tell him to leave on my own, I'm hoping he'll read into my question and excuse himself.

He shrugs. "We're just chillin today as far as I know. Probably hit the gym in a little bit."

"Oh, okay."

"Let me run something by you," he says, licking his lips.

"What's up?"

"Was this just a one-time thing for you?"

A pit forms in my stomach at the thought of never feeling him inside me again. At feeling that connection with him being a one-time thing. But continuing something with him would be a mistake. Too much potential drama.

Right?

"Umm, I thought so. Why?"

His jaw tightens even as he nods his head. "What if I didn't want it to end?"

"Rome…"

"Hear me out. Please." Rome always speaks with a calm confidence, but the slight hesitation in his voice here gives me pause. I lock eyes with him and see a vulnerability I've never felt with a partner before. Words escape me so I wrap my arm around his neck and nod for him to continue. "All I'm asking for is this trip. Let me spend the next two weeks taking the stress away from you."

"Stress?"

He sucks his teeth. "Yes, stress. I see you, Janelle. I see the toll Amerie's constant requests take on you. I saw it during the engagement party planning, and I see it now. You give her everything she asks for but who's taking care of your wants and needs?"

I sigh. "I can't." His eyes droop with disappointment and I rush to say more. "I can't give you the next two weeks. Once all the guests get here it'll be way too difficult to sneak around. We would get caught and I can't have that."

His face lights up with joy and a little hint of mischief. "Fine. Then give me one week. One week so we can go into wedding week with a little less weight on our shoulders."

I pull at my bottom lip with my teeth, considering his words. This extra week in Tulum is supposed to be all about relaxing before the big day but what if the relaxation I really need lies in the depths of Rome Martin?

"So, you're suggesting you be my very own stress ball?"

He chuckles and pulls my leg on top of his. The heat of my pussy is right against his dick. I let out a moan when I feel him harden against me, the tip slipping between my folds. He groans and clears his throat. "If that's what you want to call it. Be selfish with me. Give me all your yes's this week and I promise I'll take care of them. And you."

Be selfish with me.

Can I really do that? Say fuck it to what my sister might think, what my mom might think, and do what I want?

Rome lays a sweet kiss on the side of my mouth, bringing me back to the moment. Morning breath be damned. "So, what do you think? Can you trust me?"

My pussy purrs so loud, it drowns the sounds of my own thoughts but I know the answer is a resounding "yes", and I tell him so.

He smiles at my response and crashes his lips to mine. Another otherworldly kiss with this man. It's becoming addictive in a dangerous way. I suck his bottom lip into my mouth, drawing out a growl from him.

At some point last night, we got caught up. We were so desperate to link our bodies back together that we forgot all about the condom. It led to a long discussion about our sexual history, and we made the decision that after experiencing the bliss of having no barrier between us that we couldn't go back. We were open about the fact that neither of us have ever felt comfortable enough to do that before but something about him makes me want to jump with both feet. At least, in the bedroom. It's turning out to be a very good decision because I can't stop grinding my pussy on him with reckless abandon.

He reaches between us to spread my folds with his fingers but as two of his fingers enter me, his phone goes off. He ignores it but then it goes off three more times.

"You should check that."

His breath comes out in a huff. "Yeah." He doesn't remove his fingers, though. They continue their slow tortuous invasion. Beneath my lashes I can see him watching me even though he should be looking at his phone. I decide to give him a show and ride his hand while tweaking my nipples.

It looks like it physically hurts him to look away from me, but he only looks at his phone for a brief moment before he turns his body into me and nestles his head into the crook of my neck. A third finger joins its friends, spreading me wider. His thumb presses down on my clit while he pumps in and out of me. Fuck, I never come this fast but I'm already almost there. He must sense it because he sucks on my neck and reaches behind me to grip a handful of my ass, kneading it and forcing me to bounce harder on his fingers.

"Fuck, Rome!" I shout. My breathing becomes more erratic when he holds up his hand to show his fingers coated in my arousal.

He locks eyes with me as he sucks each of his fingers into his mouth. I grab his wrist to stop him from licking the third finger and his eyebrows pique until I suck it into my mouth. I take my time swirling my tongue around him, enjoying watching his mouth fall slightly agape.

When I release him, his gaze shifts back and forth between me and his finger in wonder. "Fucking menace," he says in awe. That torn look takes over his face again before he whispers, "I have to go."

Of all the things he could've said, I wasn't expecting that. I try to reign in my disappointment, but I know I fail when he gives me a sympathetic smile. "Oh okay. But…what about you?" I look down at his dick, trying to poke a hole in my stomach.

He shakes his head. "I'm your stress toy, remember? You don't have to worry about me." *I want to though.* He kisses my forehead. "I'll find you later, okay?"

"Okay."

He makes me walk him to the door so I can lock up behind him and before I've even gotten back into bed there's a text waiting from him.

> Rome: When I said later, I meant it, J. I know my girl misses me already.

My heart skips a beat.

> Me: Your girl? Getting a lil ahead of yourself, no?

> Rome: I was talking about your pussy *insert wink emoji* ask her, she'll tell you we go together

> Me: Lmao shut up!

> Rome: Guess I'll have to remind her later

> Me: Guess you will

Texts come in from the ladies letting me know they're officially looking for me but my thoughts keep drifting to Rome, wondering what the hell I'm going to do with him.

"Okay, get closer," Dani demands, holding her phone up to capture us all in a selfie. We're all dressed in robes awaiting our spa treatments.

When Dani grew tired of life as a model she decided to move back home to Baltimore and focus on being an entrepreneur and social media influencer. Now, she has deals with numerous beauty, fashion, and shoe brands to promote their products and she also owns a tequila business called Promesa.

The Dahlia Resort offered us a discount on our stay in exchange for her to post about the hotel on all her platforms, so she's been taking pictures and videos ever since we landed. Arnold insisted he didn't need the discount, earning an eye roll from all of us, but Dani told him she was doing it and if he didn't want the discount he could run her the difference or shut the fuck up. So, here we are.

She looks at the photo and then hands her phone off to us to approve it before creating a post and saving it in her drafts. *Never post your location until you've already left it* is her motto and she's very strict about that. No one will see a peep from our trip until we're back home.

"Okay, so after this I was thinking we could go explore the ruins and then run some errands before we meet up with the guys for our night out." Ri's voice goes up an octave with every word. She stomps her feet and claps her hands like she just announced that Yahya Abdul Mateen II is about to come out and do our massages. Leave it to her to be excited about planning every second of our day.

Dani, Evie, and I share a look then plaster identical smiles on our faces.

"Sounds great, Ri," I concede.

"Yeah, that's fine. But there needs to be some food involved between all this activity. I'd hate to ruin the fun with my hangry ways," Evie teases.

Ri rears back as if she's been slapped.

"Didn't you eat at the hotel earlier?"

The hotel offers an American breakfast or a la carte options. I missed breakfast because I spent my entire morning under Rome and my stomach is trying to make me regret that now. Thank God the spa left us a fruit platter and champagne to gorge on while we wait or else my stomach would've already embarrassed me.

Evie scoffs. "I didn't realize we were only allowed one meal a day, massa. My bad."

Ri waves off her comment with a laugh. "Sorry. That was a little OD." Evie nods. "I'm just stressed about fitting into my dress."

Her statement confuses me because Ri is a fashion designer. She literally designed and sewed her own dress, measured perfectly to her body, so how she thought she wouldn't fit into it was beyond me.

"Girl, you made that dress to fit you, not the other way around. Don't let me catch you doing something stupid like skipping meals on this trip," Dani points her finger in Ri's face while she admonishes her.

Ri grabs her finger and kisses it. "Yes, Mom." Dani wrinkles her nose at her but smiles brightly.

Turning her attention to me, I can tell Dani is in fix-it mode. "Oh, I talked to Javier, by the way. He told me there's a boutique in town that'll have the pink ribbon. I guess since the warden has us on errand duty today," she juts her thumb behind her in Ri's direction before continuing, "we can make our way there."

I forgot all about that fucking ribbon. "That's great, D. Thank you."

"Yeah, thanks D. Maybe I should've made you my Maid of Honor."

You could hear a pin drop after she let those disrespectful words fall from her lips.

From the corner of my eye, I can see Evie pulling her micro twists up into a bun and plant her hands on her hips.

Dani keeps her eyes on me trying to anticipate my next move and if she needs to step between us. As if I would ever put my hands on my sister.

I may have wanted to knock her on her ass plenty of times throughout our lives, but I've never once acted on it. That's not our relationship. Our relationship has always been one where I protect her, even though she's older, and I always bite my tongue even when I disagree with her.

When Charity Watson wanted to fight her in eleventh grade for talking to her boyfriend, I was the ninth grader who stepped in and beat her ass.

The rage I feel with her now simmers just beneath my skin. It lingers just beneath the surface, slowly scorching me from the inside out. But the feeling that closes in around me, wrapping its claws around my neck and squeezing all the air from my lungs...is hurt.

Brutal, gut-wrenching hurt.

The silence stretches between us, every second incinerating yet another thread of Ri's and my delicate relationship. Looking at the indignant glint in her eye, I fear we may be coming close to running out of threads to fray.

"Hi ladies, sorry to keep you waiting." A woman with light brown skin and dark hair pulled back into a long french braid stands in the doorway. Her eyes have tiny lines around the edges indicating a lifetime of laughter and happiness. She's very small overall, standing only at about five-foot-four, and very petite but upon closer inspection her arms are extremely toned.

She looks between all of us with a nervous smile, no doubt picking up on the energy in the room.

"Hi there, it's no problem," Dani offers, effectively breaking the tension.

The woman smiles brightly, the lines around her eyes curve even more. "I'm Sofia. I'll be one of your masseuses today. We'll get you set up in pairs in each room if you want to follow me."

Dani chimes in immediately. "I'll pair with Nelle."

Okayyyy. Wasn't expecting that.

Dani locks arms with me. Evie wraps her arm around Ri's shoulder and leads them in front of us. She looks back at me with wide eyes before disappearing around the corner.

Sofia drops Ri and Evie off in a dimly lit room before walking Dani and I further down the hallway to a bright white room filled with pink and purple flowers.

"Okay, ladies. You can disrobe and climb under the sheets here. My partner and I will be back momentarily."

The sound of the sheets rustling on our respective massage tables grates on my nerves. The last thing I want to do right now is waste my time getting a massage when the possibility of me relaxing is slim to none now.

"Hey," Dani whispers. "I'm sorry about that. She didn't mean it."

I should've known she wanted to be paired up with me to plead Ri's case. She's always been the Amerie whisperer of the group. It irritates my soul sometimes the way she coddles her; but honestly, it makes me appreciate Dani's friendship even more because though she may be high maintenance as hell, she's always down when it counts.

I take a deep breath. "Respectfully, Dani, it wouldn't matter either way. She shouldn't have said it."

"She's been intense since she got engaged and it's only getting worse the closer the wedding gets," she sighs.

"Then she should talk to me or us. I'm her sister, not her punching bag."

"I think something is going on with her, but she won't tell me."

"Well, she better tell somebody. Go sit on that lady's couch if need be."

She scrunches her nose. "What lady?"

"A therapist."

She snorts out a laugh. "Nelle, please."

Her adorable snort pulls a much needed laugh out of me. "Or that man's couch or that person's couch. Just pick a fucking couch."

Her laugh grows into a heavy wheeze. "Something is wrong with you."

"Well shit, let me lead the charge to the couches then.''

''Oh my God,'' she holds her palm up to stop me from saying anything else as she gasps for air.

Footsteps echo in the hallway and get closer to us by the second.

Dani adjusts her position and I think that's the end of our conversation, but she turns to me and says one more thing. "I feel you. I'll talk to her, okay?"

My friend shouldn't have to tell my sister to be nice to me. That shit is weird as hell, but here we are needing mediation.

"Okay."

Sofia and another woman who introduces herself as Guadalupe enter the room and tell us all about the massages they'll be giving us today before getting started.

I want to feel relaxed from Guadalupe's touch. I want to soak in the essential oils being used on my skin. I want to bask in the pampering I'm receiving, but it all just feels wrong. I can feel Guadalupe working her fingers to the bone trying to loosen the tension in my shoulders, but it's so tightly coiled it would take the jaws of life to undo.

Or Rome.

Something tells me his touch could easily take away the anxiety wrestling with my limbs.

It was strongly suggested that we leave our phones with our clothes, but I'm wound too tight for this massage so I kept mine with me, hiding it beneath my breasts. I hear Guadalupe's heavy sigh when I slip my phone from under me to beneath the table to type up a message. She knows as well as I do this massage is a waste of time.

> Me: So how does this stress relief arrangement work exactly?

The bubbles pop up almost immediately. I wonder what he and the guys are up to. Was he waiting for my text?

> Rome: Simple.

> Rome: You tell me you need me and I come

> Me: And then I come?

> Rome: *laughing emoji* Told you it was simple

> Me: I need you.

> Rome: On my way

CHAPTER FOUR

Rome

SURREAL.

That's the best word I can think of to describe how it felt to slide inside of her.

Janelle's body is a paradise that I could spend my life exploring and it still wouldn't be enough. What's more is that it felt so good to just be with her. In between all the sexing, we just talked. About everything. It's amazing how easy it is to talk to her about shit I've never told anyone.

When she texted me that she needed me, I was relieved. Thankful I wasn't alone in my hunger.

A quickie in a supply closet down the hall from the spa where she was supposed to be wasn't how I would've preferred to see her again, but the smile on her face and limp in her walk when she left made it worth it.

To be honest, I know one week with her isn't going to be enough time. Now that I've had a taste of her, I'm insatiable. There's not a chance in hell I'll be able to be around her next week and not want to fall into her warmth.

I'll take what I can get, though. She could give me literal crumbs and I would devour them like they were my last meal simply because it's her.

After my workout with the guys this morning we all went our separate ways to enjoy some free time and then decided to meet up at the pool. Right now, we're at one of the private pools that only the few located in our wing of the hotel can access. The pool is oblong shaped, encircled by plush lounge chairs and surrounded by tall trees. There's a small outdoor bar not far away from the pool and we've already become great friends with the bartender stationed there, Tomas.

Christian has spent his day flirting with every woman he's seen, and he's now brought one of them back to the pool with us. Micah is standing with Tomas at the bar while Arnold swims laps like he's training for the Olympics.

When Arnold finishes his last lap, Christian turns his attention from the woman under his arm.

"Aye, bruh, how come you don't have any activities planned for us like Amerie does for the ladies? We ain't special enough?" He laughs.

We all laugh with him. If there's one thing Christian's gonna do, it's talk shit. "Listen, I told Ri she was doing too much. This extra week is supposed to be about relaxing before all the activities we're doing with everyone next week but my lady gonna do what she gonna do and you gonna respect it."

"I see you, my boy. Learning the language of marriage already. She's always right."

Arnold rolls his eyes. "You don't know shit about marriage or women, fool."

"I think I know a thing or two about women. Ain't that right, baby?" He flashes a grin at the woman beside him, whose name we still don't know because I don't think Christian even knows, and she returns the grin tenfold.

"Maybe a little something."

I shake my head. I'm surprised Christian's even still here and not trying to convince this poor unsuspecting soul to go back to his room with him.

"What else does Ri have planned for them today?" I hope the tone of my voice is casual and not at all like I'm asking because I want to get a gauge on Janelle's schedule.

Arnold jumps out of the pool and sits on the lounge chair by me where he left his towel. "I have no clue. I can't keep it all straight, but I know she wanted all of us to go dancing tonight."

"Where at?" Christian asks.

"Does it make a difference? Yo ass gonna be there," Micah chimes in, taking a sip from his drink.

Christian sits on the lounge chair on the opposite side of me and his guest invites herself to sit on his lap. "I can't be curious? Damn. I'm down for a night out though. Shake shit up."

The woman on his lap looks at him expectantly probably for an invite to tonight's festivities and Christian is acting like he doesn't notice because I'm sure he plans to be moved on to the next one by then.

"What's your name, Miss?" I ask Christian's mystery guest. Christian doesn't care to involve her in our conversation, but I was raised right, so I will.

She smiles shyly at me. "Tiana."

"Nice to meet you. I'm Rome," I hold my hand out to shake hers and Christian looks at me like I've lost my mind, so I just chuckle at him.

"Oh, um, I know. Actually, I know who all of you are." She looks around at all of us.

"Oh, really?" Arnold asks, his voice harsh and skeptical. He never trusts anyone who claims to know us, always looking for their ulterior motive.

"Yeah. I admit I didn't recognize Chris because I'm so used to just hearing his voice but then I saw you guys when we came over here." She points to me. "Your article in Esquire was dope as hell and my niece is obsessed with your games." She turns to point at Micah. "A friend of mine put me on to your work. I went to your gallery opening a few years back." Micah nods his head with respect. She points to Arnold, who still has his eyes narrowed at her. "And you made headlines for making Jay Daniels the highest paid wide receiver in NFL history. Nobody saw that coming after his injury, but it was well deserved. I was impressed."

Well, damn. She really did know each and every one of us.

"Wait a minute," Christian interrupts. "So, you mean to tell me I was the only one you didn't recognize?" Typical Christian. He wasn't interested in a damn word this woman had to say until she wasn't fawning over him.

She chuckles. "I said I didn't recognize you at first. I don't live in Baltimore so I don't listen to your station like that, but I am a faithful listener of your podcast."

He puffs his chest out with pride. This man is really simple.

We talk to Tiana a little more and I'm surprised that Christian stumbled upon a smart woman to spend his time with when he normally likes the women who are happy sitting in silence while he chops it up like they're nothing more than life-size dolls. I'm sure this was an accident on his part, but I hope she digs her claws in him deep enough that we won't have to deal with anyone else for the rest of the trip.

Watching Christian openly flirt with Tiana makes me wish I could do the same with a certain voluptuous beauty.

"Ay, Janelle!" Christian's voice travels over my shoulder and when I turn my head, I see the woman who has completely clouded my brain.

She looks amazing in the same copper brown shorts and white tank I saw her in earlier. Her thick thighs are slick with some kind of oil, making my mans sit up a little in my shorts. When she hears her name, she stops and scans the area before she spots us and the storm clouds in her eyes tell me that someone undid all the work I did to de-stress her earlier.

She looks behind her before walking over to where Christian, Tiana, and myself are sitting.

"Hi," she says lamely.

"What's wrong with you?" Christian asks.

She looks at me briefly before sitting down beside me, careful not to let her legs touch mine. What happened between earlier and now?

She sighs. "Nothing. I'm just tired now. It's been a long day." She seems to shake herself out of her stupor enough to notice Tiana. "Hi, I'm Janelle. I love your top." She gestures toward the black mesh like top she was wearing.

"Aww, thank you. I love your hair. I'm Tiana. Nice to meet you." The two women share a warm smile between them.

Christian rolls his eyes and continues his line of questioning. "Where y'all been at all day?"

"Why, you miss us?" We all turn to Eve who somehow snuck up on us.

"It depends, did you miss me?" He licks his lips when he asks the question, causing Eve to stick her finger in her mouth, pretending to gag. I think he enjoys flirting with her because she genuinely doesn't like him. He thinks he can get under her skin and worm his way into her panties just to say he did it, but to flirt with her while another woman sits on your lap is bold even for him.

Tiana doesn't look put off by it at all, though. I think she has her own motives for spending time with Christian.

"Please, the day I miss you will be the day I strap weights to my ankles and jump in the ocean."

"You play too much."

"Who's playing?"

Janelle cuts into the conversation before these two can really get started. "Anyway, we did the spa today. After that, we went to explore the ruins, then we went to look for some specific flower Ri really wanted to get from here for the wedding, and now we're about to do some other errand for her before we all go out tonight."

They crammed a lot into their morning while the guys and I did nothing. From what Arnold has told me and the little glimpses I've gotten from Janelle, I knew Amerie was a type A personality, but I wasn't expecting her to have an itinerary for every moment of every day.

A glass appears between Janelle and I, and we both look up to find Micah holding out a Mezcalita for her and a Bay Breeze for Eve.

"Y'all look like y'all could use a drink."

Eve gives Micah a seductive smile, and he just laughs before walking back over to the bar and scanning the pool area.

"Thank you, Micah." Janelle and Eve swoon in unison.

"Kiss ass!" Christian yells with his fist wrapped around his mouth.

Eve turns a scowl on him and points her glass in his direction. "Just because you wouldn't know home training if it looked your stupid ass in the mouth." She turns to Tiana. "Speaking of home training—Hi, I'm Evie. You're gorgeous."

"Oh my gosh, you're so sweet. I'm Tiana."

"Can I give you a piece of advice, Tiana?"

"Sure," she says.

"No," Christian says at the same time.

"Run far away from this one. Unless you wanna leave this vacation with something you can't get rid of, if you know what I'm saying." She winks.

"Now you lying on my dick? That's foul, Evelyn."

Eve ignores him. "You know, if you're looking for a fine ass man to pass the time with, sans the community dick, I got you. I've made some connections while here. Oh my gosh, you should come out with us tonight." She starts talking excitedly and Tiana starts matching her energy. Before we know it, the two women are up and out of their seats walking out of the pool area, and Christian is following behind them whining for attention.

Janelle shakes her head with a laugh. "I swear those two couldn't exist without the other one to torture."

"I'm telling you they're gonna be the next ones walking down the aisle the way they bicker."

"I highly doubt it. Evie cannot stand Christian. It's not a facade."

"I know but hate fucking is a real thing and the sexual tension is off the charts."

"We see it as sexual tension, but I think we may be on the verge of being witnesses to a homicide. She says he reminds her of her hoe ass daddy who she also can't stand, so she really isn't fucking with him."

"Damn. Thought I had another best man title on lock. I guess I'll have to give his eulogy instead."

She turns to me with a shocked expression that dissolves into hysterics, holding her side from the laughter. "And I guess I'ma have to put money on Evie's books."

"We'll get her set up real nice. She'll have all the honey buns **and** ramen."

She must forget about her desire to put distance between us because she plants her hand on my knee trying to gain control of her laugh. It feels good to have her hands on me.

Dani walks by the pool area but notices our group and steps in to say hi. "Dani, where's my wife?"

"She's not your wife yet, stop trying to claim my woman early. *My* woman is changing, said she got too hot in her outfit." She lifts her head to make eye contact with Janelle. "She's gonna be looking for us soon, I'm sure."

"I'm sure," she mumbles under her breath, but keeps a smile on her face as she nods.

Dani looks at Micah, but only briefly, before she averts her eyes and walks out of the pool area. From the corner of my eye, I see Micah set his drink down and follow her out.

I'll have to ask him what that's about later.

Arnold jumps out of the pool, probably to go find Amerie before she sets off on her next adventure, leaving me and Janelle alone in the lounge chair.

I nudge Janelle's shoulder with my own. "So, what's up? You seemed down when you first walked by."

The whiskey brown orbs of her eyes drink me in as she takes a sip of her drink. "I'm just tired. It's been nonstop all day today and it's driving me up the wall. This week was supposed to be about relaxation. Every detail of this wedding was handled before we even stepped on the plane, and yet she keeps coming up with more stuff to do. I know I sound ungrateful right now."

She's probably thinking that because Arnold paid for us to be here this extra week. We all told him he didn't need to do that, but he insisted it was his gift to us for being in the wedding party.

"You're allowed to be tired, J. What is it you want to be doing right now?"

"Honestly? I just wanted to sit by the pool and read. Or sit on the beach and read. Water and books, that's all I want."

"Do that, then."

"You heard Dani. Ri will be looking for us soon to run more errands."

"Tell her no."

She sighs. "I can't do that."

"Why?"

"Because," she pauses. "She's my sister. I just want her to have a good time, no stress."

"So, you'll just take all the stress on yourself?"

She bumps her leg against mine. "That's why I have a new stress toy, isn't that what you said?"

I snicker at her joke, but I wish I could make her put herself first sometimes when it comes to her sister. Just because it's her wedding doesn't mean she gets to take advantage of Janelle.

"That is true. Stress relief reporting for duty." I give her a tiny salute and she throws her head back in laughter.

"You about to get me in trouble." Her eyes travel the length of my body, biting her bottom lip as she does.

"Why is that, J?"

"Because if I had more time, I would squeeze you right now."

We look at each other intently then burst out laughing.

"Ayo, what?"

She forces her words out between her chortles. "I swear that sounded better in my head. I was trying to make a joke like squeeze you like a stress toy. Get it?"

"Ohh okay, so you want to squeeze my stress balls. Got it."

"Oh God, now it's getting worse."

"You started it. Talking about squeeze me like I'm Pillsbury Doughboy or something."

"Please. I can't breathe." Her laughs turn into a wheeze. "You don't squeeze the Pillsbury Doughboy; you poke him in the belly. Like this." She demonstrates by poking me straight in my belly button.

I swat her hand. "You're on thin ice."

She puts her hands up in surrender, humor still lighting up her features. "Okay, okay. My bad. Thank you, though."

"For what?"

"For this arrangement. Being with you really is helping my stress levels. I just don't want to put all my shit on your plate, so you have to tell me if you want to cut it early. I won't be offended."

But I would be. Hell, we're already cutting it early by limiting ourselves to one week. She really has no idea the effect she has on me in such a short period of time.

"J, I wouldn't be doing this with you if I didn't want to. Believe me, I am enjoying the hell out of this and you. So, load my plate. I can handle it."

She giggles. "I can do that."

We start talking about how the spa treatments went after I left when we hear a voice.

"Nelle." Janelle jumps away from me like she was just caught doing something inappropriate. We turn to find Dani waving in our direction. "You ready to go?"

"Yeah, I'm ready." She stands up and puts a respectable amount of distance between us before meeting my eyes again. "I'll see you later?"

"Of course."

She nods and walks over to Dani, grabbing her hand and pulling her away from the pool area.

I rub my hands down my face.

That woman is going to be the death of me, and I will welcome it like an old friend when it comes.

I stand up to make my way to my room, stopping to make a few phone calls on my way. If Janelle won't do things for herself then I'll do them for her.

Arnold: Everyone meet in the lobby in ten minutes

Christian: Ima need more than ten fam

Arnold: …

Micah: Please tell me you're not texting while having sex

Christian: What do you wanna hear?

Micah: I thought Tiana ditched you for Eve

Christian: Who said anything about Tiana?

Arnold: You got thirty minutes or your ass is getting left

Christian: I can make that work

Me: That ain't the flex you think it is

Christian: *middle finger emoji*

Knowing that the guys are occupied, I switch over to my text thread with Janelle.

Me: You alone?

Her reply is damn near instant.

J: Yeah why?

I don't need to hear anything else. I shove my phone in my pocket and head out to Janelle's room. When I get to her hallway, she's walking to her door with what looks like a candy bar in hand. She looks good as hell. She's wearing a white crop top that stops just below her breastbone. Her silver belly button ring stands out against her brown skin and the gold waist beads adorning her torso. Her white skirt is ruched at the top and the right side flows to her ankle while the left side sits completely open, showing off another gold chain wrapped around her thigh. My mouth waters at the sight of her.

I rush over and wrap my hand around her waist, slamming her back against her door.

Her eyes widen at my touch and widen even more when she sees it's me, but once I press the weight of my leg between her thighs, they relax into a lustful gaze.

"Rome, what the hell do you think you're doing?" She teases her bottom lip with her teeth and looks around the empty hallway.

"I wanted to see you." I bury my head into the crook of her neck and lick a trail up the base. She squirms under my touch, grinding against my leg. She lets her exposed thigh fall open slightly exposing her pretty pussy covered with a strip of lace.

"Mmm, oh my God, are you trying to get us caught?"

"Would it really matter if we did?" I'm talking out of my ass right now, allowing my need for her to take over my common sense. I know she doesn't want to get caught with me and I know why, but it doesn't change the fact that being with her feels so damn good. And right.

"Rome. You don't want the shit storm that would be people finding out about us any more than I do."

Now, that's where she's wrong. I had reservations in the beginning but the moment I slid between her thighs they melted away. I would announce our relationship, if you can call it that, to the world.

"Word?" She averts her eyes, but I grab her chin and force her to look at me. "Nah, look me in my eyes 'cause I wanna make sure you hear me. I'm a grown ass man, J. I'm not afraid of getting caught. The only reason I'm hiding shit from anyone is because it's what you want."

She stares deep into my eyes and licks her lips. "Okay, that's fair. We have a few minutes. Do you want to come inside?"

Absolutely. But I also want her to be as desperate for me as I am for her, so instead of letting her open her door and guide us inside, I place her legs firmly on the ground and take a step back.

"Nah, like I said I just wanted to see you. I don't want to mess up your outfit before you have a chance to show it off."

"What?" Her brows furrow and she tilts her head to try to make sense of what I just said.

"I'll see you downstairs, J." I pull her into me for a quick kiss before I turn around and walk back to my room.

Mystical Nightclub is one of the biggest nightclubs in the Tulum area. The bar consumes the entire back wall of the club with about five bartenders on duty. The VIP tables line the perimeter behind the DJ booth and wrap around looking down on the large dance floor. Outside, there's another bar, another dance floor, and a hookah lounge.

When we walk in, Janelle and the other women capture the attention of everyone. They're all wearing all white outfits, I'm sure coordinated by Amerie, and have an aura about them that says they're not to be fucked with.

I catch a lot of eyes lingering on Janelle, but it doesn't bother me. You'd have to be blind not to notice how beautiful she is.

I recognize Tiana from earlier, when she runs up to give Eve and Janelle hugs, pulling a tall dark skin man along behind her. I turn to see if Christian is bothered but he's already sizing up the room to find his next target.

A hostess leads us to a VIP table and gives the women glowstick bracelets and the men chains with glowsticks hanging from them. A bottle girl brings out a bottle of Promesa tequila on ice and a bottle of Dusse along with glasses. Arnold grabs the bottle of Dusse and Amerie grabs the bottle of Promesa. They pour glasses for everyone and hand them out to us before raising their own.

"To a night we'll never forget to kick off a life we'll never regret," Amerie cheers. Everyone cheers with her and takes their shots. My eyes connect with Janelle's and she never takes her eyes off me as she downs her shot of tequila with no chaser. I smile around my glass as I let the brown liquid burn my throat.

The DJ announces it's "Blackout Night" at the club tonight which means that at random points throughout the night, the inside of the club will go completely dark and the only thing you'll be able to see is the shine of the glowsticks. He then goes back to his playlist and when WizKid and Tem's "Essence" comes on, Eve drags Janelle and Dani out to the dance floor. Amerie does the same with Arnold, but guides him a little further away from the other women.

A red light blinks throughout the club three times and then the room is bathed in darkness. A few people shout with excitement and then the DJ starts to play Usher's "Good Kisser". I can barely see in front of me so I certainly can't see anything happening on the dance floor. The only way I'm able to see the glass in my hand is because of the green glowstick hanging from my neck.

He mixes the song with a few afrobeats. With the lights off, the energy in the room is almost palpable. Everyone is intrigued with what can be done in the dark.

We stay in the dark for a little while longer and then that same red light starts flashing again but this time, I notice it flashes ten times before the lights come back on. I watch as we collectively adjust to the change, even though the lights aren't bright at all.

Christian, who I never even saw leave our section, comes back with three women in tow. Two of them try talking to Micah and I but we show no interest in them so they turn their efforts back to Christian. Micah pours himself another glass of Dusse, and I hold out my glass for him to fill mine as well. "You not interested in Christian's trappings tonight?" He questions.

"Nah, you know I'm never up for his fuck shit." I find Janelle in the crowd, whining her hips to the music. Her movements are like water, flowing effortlessly to the beat. Right now, her, Eve, and Dani are all dancing together in a circle, but my focus never leaves Janelle. I'm in a trance only she can free me from, but I hope she consumes me instead.

"Word of advice, bruh. If you're trying to hide whatever's going on with you and Janelle, you might not wanna stare at her like she's your next meal."

Micah's words snap me out of the moment. I turn toward him and catch the childlike grin on his face. "What you mean?"

"It's obvious you two got something going on. How long?"

I rub my hand against my beard. I know Janelle doesn't want anyone to know, but Micah is the person I'd trust the most with this besides my brother, Jalen. I don't see a point in lying to him. "It just happened last night. It's just supposed to be a friends with benefits situation this week."

"Just for the week? Interesting."

"Interesting? What's interesting?"

"Nothing at all."

I'm not even going to bother trying to decipher his meaning. He sees too much as it is. "You don't think this shit is crazy? With her being Arnold's ex and all?"

"It's no crazier than Arnold ending up with Amerie, and I don't think the two of them together is crazy at all." He shrugs.

I nod my head in agreement. Even if I think it's shady that Arnold ended up with his ex's sister, it kept Janelle in my life so I can't be too upset. "Aight, so what about you? Since we exposing shit we've noticed and all, I did catch some weird vibes between you and Dani. What's up?"

At my comment, he turns to watch Dani grinding her ass against some man on the dance floor. "I wish I knew." He shakes his head and stands. "I'm gonna go hit this hookah. You coming?"

Looking back at Janelle, I take note of the color of the glowsticks on her wrists. Blue. They're all blue. "I'm good for now."

"Bet." Micah heads down the steps and out to the lounge area. Christian is fully engrossed with his three companions, so I head down to the dance floor.

I walk a straight path past Janelle and my hand graces her lower back as I pass. I can feel her skin prickle beneath my touch. I love how easily my touch affects her.

When I get to the bar, I don't order anything, I just lean against it, pretending to take in the crowd. I see Dani move deeper into the crowd, dancing with someone new. Eve grabs the guy she was dancing with and pulls him to the bar.

That red light starts flashing again and I make deliberate eye contact with Janelle just as the lights go off.

I waste no time following the four blue lights until our bodies are flush together. I reach my hand out to feel for her stomach and when I do I tug on her waist beads, slipping my finger beneath them to caress her bare skin.

"Hi," her voice is breathy and full of need.

I lift my hands to feel for her face and when I find it, I lean down and place a kiss on the side of her mouth. "Hi."

The song switches to Zeina's "Nasty" and Janelle slides her hands beneath my shirt, dragging her nails down my abs. I hiss at the contact and grab her hips. I can't see her face but I can feel the urgency in her movements. When Zeina starts singing about being anxious for your love, she turns her body, planting her ass firmly against my groin and starts rotating her body. I square my feet, pushing one hand against the arch in her back and the other on her ass so that I can match her rhythm. I can't hide my dick growing hard behind her and I don't try to. I want her to feel me. I can feel her body shudder in my hands.

She rolls her body back so that her back is plush to my chest, leaning her head back into my shoulder. My hands trace up and down her thighs, but when my fingers brush the end of her skirt slit, I hear her gasp. Her hand slams down on top of mine and moves it closer to the thin line of her panties.

I lean down to whisper in her ear.

"Tell me what you need, J."

"I need to come," she whispers.

"I got you."

I push her panties to the side and slide my fingers into her wetness. She's soaked already and it makes my dick even harder to know all this is for me. Her head flies back into my chest again as she grinds down on my fingers, while still somehow keeping up with the beat of the song.

I cup my hand so that my three fingers can pump in and out of her while my thumb presses on her clit to make her come out and play. If I thought we'd have enough time, I'd drop to my knees to lap her up, but this will just have to be enough for now.

Her movements become more erratic, falling out of tune from the beat. The only music we can hear is our sharp breathing. I can tell she's about to come when her legs start tensing up, so I use my free hand to wrap around her throat and pull her head back to face me. As her release starts to coat my hand, I slam my lips to hers and swallow her moans whole.

That red light starts to blink so even though the last thing I want to do is leave her, I steady her on her feet, put her panties back in place, and plant a quick kiss on her neck before walking away.

When the lights come back on, I'm standing at the bar and Janelle is looking around the crowd. She spots Dani and calls her back over and the two start talking and dancing.

I order Janelle's drink of choice from the bartender and when he hands me the Mezcalita I turn back to find Janelle in the same place I left her. Eve has rejoined the group and is whispering in Dani's ear so Janelle sneaks a look in my direction.

I take my finger, still coated in her release and dip it in my drink, stirring it around. Her eyes widen at the sight and when I hold my glass up to her and wink, her jaw goes slack.

The taste of her is exactly what this drink was missing.

CHAPTER FIVE

Janelle

L AST NIGHT WAS UNBELIEVABLE AND UNFORGETTABLE. LETTING, NO demanding, Rome make me come in the middle of the dance floor where the lights could've come up at any moment to expose us is the most reckless thing I've done in a while. It was also the most freeing. I knew Rome would not only get me where I needed to go but also keep me safe while doing it.

When he made a show of using his arousal covered finger to stir his drink, I almost dragged him to the bathroom to finish what we started. Instead, I watched him go to the bathroom alone before I went to the ladies' room and got myself together. We spent the rest of the night dancing with each other and everyone else; except it didn't escape my notice that Ri kept herself and Arnold in their own little corner. She seems to have fed into our mom's bullshit notion that I am hung up on her soon-to-be husband and wants to keep me away from him.

What does it say about our relationship that she thinks I'd actually try something with her man?

Do I seem like that kind of person?

I purse my lips at my sister's obvious mistrust, but then a still sleeping Rome pulls me in closer to him and the warmth of his body takes away the tension in my bones.

We stayed at Mystical Nightclub until they closed at three a.m. and Rome wasted no time coming to my room after we all separated. I have no idea what time we went to bed but I'm too wired to attempt to sleep now.

Careful not to wake Rome, I turn in his arms so I can take him in fully. His lashes are impossibly long; each one is perfectly curved. His right eyebrow has a slight kink in it. It's a minor imperfection that only adds to his overall allure. His bottom lip is only slightly bigger than his top lip, moisturized and ready to be kissed. I almost want to reach my hand up and trace them, but I don't want to risk waking him. When he's awake, Rome has a menacing look to him. The sharp lines of his jaw and harsh eyes make him look sexy as hell, but also like he might kill you if you cross him. Sleeping, though, he looks so peaceful. Gentle even.

He looks like mine.

"You got your fill? Or should I turn to give you another angle?"

I jump at the sound of his voice and slap him in the chest when he opens his eyes, wiggling his eyebrows at me.

"Ass. How long have you been up?"

"You mean how long have I noticed you staring at my skin like you wanna wear it? A while."

I playfully shove him in the chest again and try to roll away, but he grabs me by the waist and holds tight. "I can't stand you. You should've told me to stop being a creep sooner."

"Nah, I like when you look at me."

Sleeping with this man was a terrible idea. Not only does he have a stroke game that will have you sitting in the bushes outside his house waiting for him to show his face but he says things that feel real and permanent.

It's not. This is a fantasy we're selling each other.

He is a damn good salesman though.

"Let me find out you're needy."

"And if I am? What you gonna do about it?" He nuzzles his head against my breasts while massaging my hip dimples.

It's hard to think straight with him clouding my space like this so I change the subject. "Do you have to sneak out soon?"

"Nope. I'm free today, and so are you." He slides out from under the covers and heads to the bathroom. I lean forward in the bed so I can peek into the bathroom to see that he's using the spare toothbrush provided by the hotel and helping himself to my toothpaste.

"How you figure that? You know Ri probably has our day planned down to the minute. I gotta ask her for bathroom breaks."

He doesn't answer for a while, the sounds of water running and him brushing his teeth filling the room. When I hear the sink turn off, I get up to head in and brush my own teeth and I find him scrubbing his face with a washcloth and my face cleanser. He sure got comfortable in my space very fast.

"I figure that because whatever plans you have today, I need you to get out of them."

Scoffing, I step by him to grab my toothpaste from the edge of the sink. He meets my eyes in the mirror and I'm taken aback by the lack of humor I see on his face. His eyes are low and his jaw is tight. He's serious? "Rome, how the hell am I supposed to get out of whatever Ri has planned today? I'm the maid of honor, that's not a good look."

"What did I ask you to do when we first agreed to do this whole thing?" He motions his hands between us.

My mind flashes back to the morning after our first night together. It feels like weeks have passed since I turned my life upside down for him instead of mere days. Chewing on my bottom lip, I let out a sigh. "To give you all my yes's."

"And that I would take care of them and you. Right. So, you know I wouldn't ask you to do this if I didn't have your best interest at heart."

"I know."

"Then can you please just trust me?"

I do trust him, completely, and that terrifies me because it's not in my nature. My dad taught me to never give anyone my trust until they've earned it, so how the hell is it possible that Rome could have earned my trust in three days? Sure, I've known him for almost two years before this trip, but this is the first time we're really spending extended periods of time together, alone.

I'm confused as hell and I don't know what to make of the man in front of me, but I find myself walking past him to grab my phone anyway.

> Me: I need y'all to do me a favor

> Evie: It's so early for favors

Me: Girl you think it's too early for everything

Evie: And yet you ask anyway

Dani: No you bitches are not blowing up my phone when I'm barely conscious

Evie: Blowing up your phone? It was four texts. Dramatic

Dani: One is too many. The vibrations are so loudddddd

Dani: But what you need Nelle?

Me: I need Ri interference

Dani: What you mean?

Me: I can't handle any outings right now I just need a day of silence

Evie: Omg love her down but she will have to pry my cold dead body out of this room if she wants to do stuff today I'm not with it

Dani: LMAO I feel that my battery is all the way dead

Evie: Let her spend some time with her man and leave us be

Dani switches over to the group chat with all four of us on it to ask Ri to pardon us from activity today and Ri reluctantly agrees. I could've texted her myself but I knew it would go over better coming from anyone but me.

Satisfied with my efforts, I turn to Rome with a wide smile on my face. He looks good as hell leaning against the bathroom door jam in nothing but his briefs shaking his head in utter amusement.

"You good?"

"I'm great. So, what are we doing with all this free time?" I start to saunter toward him and he meets me halfway, dropping his lips to mine in a sweet kiss.

"You'll see. Now get dressed. Wear a bathing suit." He turns his back to me and starts pulling on the clothes he wore last night. "I'm gonna go shower and grab my stuff, but I'll meet you back here in thirty."

Hold on, get dressed? Wear a bathing suit? When he demanded I free up my day, I assumed he wanted to spend the entire day in bed. I wasn't expecting an outing and now I'm even more turned around.

It's risky because after I just made a big deal out of wanting to stay in all day to the girls it would be wild for me to get caught out and with Rome no less, but the idea of spending quality time with him outside of these four walls has a whole stampede of elephants running rampant in my stomach.

"Umm, okay."

"No questions?"

"Were there supposed to be? I thought you told me to just trust you."

"I'm just impressed you're listening. Let me find out you're a good girl after all."

Heat rushes to my core, leaving me breathless. "Keep playing, you'll find out what a good girl I am."

His gaze travels the length of my body so painstakingly slowly I can feel all the womanism jumping out of my skin.

He lets out a sarcastic huff and bends down to grab my bag. He claims to have already packed it with the essentials at some point this morning. I'm convinced the man never sleeps. "Thirty minutes, Janelle."

"Favorite animal."

As promised, Rome came back to my room after thirty minutes and led me to one of our rental cars. We've all typically been riding bikes into town since it's not far, so the fact that we're in the rental means we're going further than the hotel provided bike rentals would take us. What is he up to?

We've been driving for the past ten minutes, and I've been asking random questions to keep from asking that exact question.

"A giraffe," he says after a moment.

"Aww, forreal? Giraffes are cute. Did you know that giraffes are the largest terrestrial animal?"

He laughs and drops his hand to my thigh. "I didn't know that. Look at you coming through with the animal facts."

"Had to show you I'm more than just a pretty face."

"I think I knew that already, Dr. Cross." I smile at his jab. "Okay, what's your favorite animal?"

"Oh, easy. Turtles."

"Turtles? I wasn't expecting that."

"Turtles are probably one of the most adorable animals to exist. Especially sea turtles, their shells are so beautiful."

"And hit me with an animal fact because I know you want to."

"Oh, well, I fuck with sea turtles heavy because they're loners. They actually rarely interact with each other unless they're mating and I respect that, because if you're not clapping these cheeks why are you in my space?"

"Wowww, you said close the door on your way out."

"Periodt. Not you, though. I might like you in my space just a little bit. For now."

"Only a little bit? I gotta work on that."

"There's always room for improvement."

"Noted. Do you consider yourself a loner forreal? You don't come across that way to me."

"Oh, but I am. My circle is very small. Outside of Ri, Evie, and Dani, I'm friendly with the other doctors at my practice but that's about it. I'm what I like to call an extroverted introvert. Yes, I know ambivert is a word, but I like my way better. I can be very social but I'm mainly only that way with my friends and when my social battery dies, it dies."

"Damn, so me and the guys aren't your friends?"

"Arnold definitely isn't my friend, not anymore. Micah and Christian, yeah okay. I hang out with them. But I didn't see you hitting me up for shit prior to this trip, sir."

He rolls his eyes. "I had my reasons for that."

"And what were they? Because after we met the first time you kept your distance and I thought damn he really doesn't fuck with me. When we planned the engagement party together, I thought we had fun but even then you were distant. This new version of you that wants to dick me down and spend time with me? It's taken some getting used to."

"It's not a new version of me. It's the real me. I'm just not holding back anymore."

"Why were you in the first place?"

"Maybe one day I'll tell you. Just know, you've never been the problem."

I didn't realize how much I needed to hear that until he said it. I want to press him for the details but I don't want to push him past his limits. I'll let him tell me when he's ready. I pout my lips and nod my head. "Hmm okay. Fine. Keep your secrets."

"Thank you. And I get what you were saying, too. I love spending time with my friends and family. I'm always down for an adventure with them, but I'm really in my bag when I can just zone out and work on a project by myself. Conferences, interviews, and things like that? Completely drain me."

"See, look at that. You're more like a sea turtle than you thought."

"Who would've thought?"

"The more you know," I say, spreading my hands out to represent a rainbow. He tickles the inside of my thigh, making me bend over with laughter.

"You know you can swim with sea turtles here, right? Is that on the agenda for this week?"

My smile drops and I tear my eyes away from him. "It somehow didn't make the cut."

He cuts his eyes over to me and lets them linger before turning his attention back to the road. "Can I ask what's up with you and your sister? I know you said it's not about Arnold, but what is it about? Because you can't tell me something isn't up."

I shift in my seat so that my right knee is up against the door with my foot under my ass. "Ri is my best friend, or at least she used to be. I don't know—shit between us has been weird for a minute now, before she started dating Arnold but her being with him has personified it. I don't get it."

"You don't wanna ask her?"

"I have asked her. She insists that I'm reading everything wrong and that we have no issues, but it doesn't feel that way."

I keep making the excuse for her that wedding planning is just stressing her out, but that excuse is paper thin and the words on the page fade more and more with every shot she takes at me.

"It doesn't look that way either."

I clear my throat and look out of the window. "Are you and your brother close?" I haven't met Jalen Martin yet since he wasn't able to make it to the engagement party, but Rome has mentioned him plenty of times.

"Extremely. That's my guy. I was always his shadow growing up, because he's four years older than me and now his son is my little shadow."

"That's adorable. Does he play any of your games?"

"Oh yeah, you can't tell his little ass he's not a pro gamer. *Proving Grounds* exists solely because he challenged me to create it."

Proving Grounds was one of Downhill Studios most popular games last year. It's a horror game set in a zombie apocalypse where the player must fight their way through an infested city and is only given a certain timeframe to do so. His company was already a giant in the videogame industry, but this game quickly became one of the top-rated zombie games next to *The Last of Us*, the *Resident Evil* franchise, and *Left 4 Dead*.

"Wait, you still design the games? I assumed you were too busy running the place to do that."

"Game design is still my heart even though I don't get to do it as much anymore. That was a special project for Kam, so I had to."

"You're a good uncle."

"I try to be." My ovaries keep trying to speak up as if I want to hear anything they have to say. *Pipe the fuck down.*

"I can't believe you really designed *Proving Grounds*. That game gave me nightmares," I chuckle.

"Hold the fuck up. You played the game?"

"Yeah, Evie made me. She knows I don't like horror games, but she insisted this one was fire. She wasn't wrong. Still terrified me though."

He laughs and rubs his hand over his beard before gripping my thigh again. "I didn't know you and Eve were gamers."

She keeps it under wraps, but Evie is a huge gamer. She has an entire YouTube channel dedicated to speed runs of her favorite games. I'm not on her level, and I usually spend my free time reading but I have been known to lose myself in games from time to time. "Stick around, you might learn a thing or two about me."

"I plan to."

A charged silence falls over the car, steeped in unspoken claims and false promises.

One week.

That's all we have.

"We're here." His claim jolts me back to the present. When I look up, I see that we're at a dock and there's a group of three people waving to us from a very large boat.

I turn to Rome with my jaw on the ground. "What is going on?"

"You've been saying that you just wanted to read by the water. I figured if we went to the pool, we'd just be interrupted and you'd be dragged into yet another activity. So," he waves toward the yacht, "I brought the water to you."

I look back and forth from him to the boat several times trying to make sense of his words.

"You…you rented an entire yacht…just so I could read by the water?"

He holds up the tote bag he packed for me and hands it over so I can see my Kindle and both paperbacks I packed resting comfortably inside.

"I did. You ready?"

Ready to go half on a baby with your fine ass? Shit, put me down as a possible. *Damn these fucking ovaries.* "Y-yeah."

He puts his hand on my lower back to lead me up the dock and onboard where the captain introduces herself as Shirrelle, and the other two crew members introduce themselves as Paul and Luis. Luis gives us a tour of the ship from the two bedrooms and bathrooms to the very spacious sundeck and tells us the plan for docking so we can use the swimming platform if we want. Paul tells us what time to expect lunch and then they leave us in the downstairs lounge area.

"Rome, this is amazing. Thank you." I'm blown away by this gesture. According to the Forbes Forty Under Forty article that was done on him, Rome's net worth is in the millions. To some, dropping at least fifteen-hundred dollars on a yacht rental that could easily fit twenty to fifty people on it might seem like a drop in the bucket for him, and I'm sure it is, but the intention behind the gesture speaks volumes as to who he is and I'm listening intently.

"You're welcome. You happy you trusted me?"

"Listen, you'll get no questions from me going forward."

His laughter resonates right in my belly. "Somehow, I doubt that."

"You tryna say I'm difficult?" I slap my hand against my chest.

"Challenging," he leans down to whisper in my ear. "In the best way."

Without waiting for a response from me, he grabs my hand and pulls me over to the comfortable sofa in the lounge area. While I'm dying to open the book I haven't had time to read since I started it weeks ago, I don't make a move to pull it out of my bag. My focus keeps drifting to this enigma of a man, wondering how the hell we got here and how we'll ever go back to the status quo.

He starts to walk away but I clutch his hand.

"Wait."

"What's up?"

"Where are you going?"

His chest rumbles with a low laugh. "Leaving you to read as planned."

When I don't say anything he sits beside me on the sofa, man-spreading as he does, and leans his arm against the back of my seat. "J?"

I swallow my next words in a big gulp and turn to face him. "Yeah?"

"I didn't bring you here to entertain me. I brought you here so you could relax…properly. So, go ahead and pull out your book and ignore me for whatever fictional world you're jumping into."

"I feel so bad, though."

"Because?"

"Because you did all this for me and I'm about to forget about your entire existence once I crack open that book. What are you gonna do?"

His jaw tenses. "First of all, you need to stop worrying about other people for a second. You don't have to repay people for every little thing they do for you. The people who really fuck with you don't give a shit about that. Second, if you're so worried about how I'm gonna spend my time on this boat, run me a book then."

My brow piques. "What?"

"Let me hold one of your books so I can read with you."

"You wanna read with me?"

He lifts his eyebrow to match mine. "You don't think I can read?"

"I mean, hey, I wasn't there with you in school. I don't know what you know and don't know." He pinches and tickles me on the sides, making me fall over with tears of laughter. "Okay! Okay! I'm just saying I mostly read romance so I wasn't sure if you knew what you were getting yourself into. Although, I do read thrillers too. I have the latest Ciara Jeffries release with me if you wanna read that."

"Mhm. What are you reading right now?"

"I'm reading the second book in this series by A.R. Washington. It's a fake dating book which is one of my favorite tropes. I started it a few weeks ago, but between work, research, and helping Ri with wedding stuff, I haven't had a chance to go back to it. I've been fiending for it though because the man is already a top tier book boyfriend and I need another dose." I cut myself off because I can hear my voice becoming too high-pitched to understand. Once you get me started on books, I can go on forever.

"The first book is about the same couple?"

"No. They're interconnected standalones. The series is about these three nurses who are all best friends and work at the same hospital. The first book in the series is about one of the other friends and the doctor she works with so it's a little forbidden."

"You have that one with you?"

"It's on my Kindle, yeah."

"Give me that one, then."

He holds his hand out, expectantly. What in the entire fuck is going on? If there's one thing I'm learning about Rome, though, it's to not underestimate him, so I reach into my bag and pull out my Kindle. Once I have the book he asked for pulled up, I turn it over to him. The cover shows a couple in scrubs standing back-to-back, but the tops of their heads are cut off.

He studies it for a moment and then pushes my sternum so I'm leaning all the way back against the couch and lifts my legs so I'm resting comfortably on the sectional portion. Then he lays his head in my lap.

I guess the conversation is over.

Grabbing my paperback, I open it to where I left off and though I'm immediately immersed back into the story, Rome's presence breaches the hub of my consciousness. I notice every shift in his body against mine. I notice every time he swipes to a new page, every sound he makes, every crease in his forehead. I even notice him highlighting a few things as he reads.

Not once does he interrupt me or try to get my attention, so I give him the same courtesy and keep to myself.

We sit in comfortable silence, devouring our books as I notice he's just as fast of a reader as I am. My hand stays planted on his head, massaging his scalp, only removing it to turn the pages.

After I read the last page of my book, I close it with a smile and stretch my arms up to the ceiling.

"Are you taking a break?"

"I just finished."

He jolts up from his seat and turns to me. "Okay good, because I have questions."

His quick movement makes me choke on my laughter and he uses his heavy ass hand to pat me on the back. "Are you not liking it?"

"I wanna know why Jharrel thought Essence was gonna come see him after he talked to her crazy in the operating room. She should've punched him dead in his shit."

"Yeah, he's an asshole."

"That's it? He's an asshole? J, this man showed up to play basketball with her brother tryna get information on her from him. Tyree should've dunked on his ol' goofy wanna be Jackson Avery head ass."

"Not you getting invested in these characters."

"I'm all the way invested because something ain't right with that man. On a brighter note, Essence is nasty. She a freak freak and I love it. I see why you like this book. It's sexy. I think I'm halfway through and shit is getting wild."

"In that case, I'm about to really put you on, make you a certified filth pusher."

"Well shit, put me on then. I'm ready."

We both laugh and I lean my head on his shoulder. "By the way, A.R. is a local writer, too. Her name's Aniyah and her brother owns that bookstore, Bookmarked and Busy, off North Charles."

"Oh yeah, I've seen that store. Have you met her?"

"No, I just follow her on socials."

"I'm gonna follow her after I get through these books. I wanna know why Tracy keeps dealing with her man when everybody knows he's cheating on her. That security guard, what's his name? Eric? He's feeling her."

I bend over in hysteria at his assessment. "Look at you thinking you know something. Tracy's book is the third book."

"And is her guy Eric?"

"It's not out yet. You gon have to wait and see."

"Mhm. I bet it is. That means I'ma have to deal with her bum ass man through all of book two I bet. Lawd."

We spend another few minutes talking about the books when Paul comes in to let us know lunch is ready, and we let him know we'd like to eat out on the sundeck.

I decide to strip down to my bathing suit because after lunch I'm going to be ready for a swim. When my shorts hit the ground, so does Rome's jaw.

This bathing suit leaves very little to the imagination. It's a jade green two-piece with a drawstring thong bottom and bikini string top.

I've never subscribed to the idea that just because you're bigger than what society deems acceptable you shouldn't be able to flaunt your body. I'm a big girl. I'm not very top heavy, I only wear a C cup bra. My waist is somewhat trimmer, but my wide hips make up for it. I've got stretchmarks, dimples, and dips on my ass and hips. My arms are flabby, my lower belly has a pooch to it, and my thighs rub together when I walk. I make no attempts to cover up because I feel very comfortable in my body, and from the way Rome is devouring me with his eyes, he agrees with me.

I look good as hell.

"Damn, J. I can't even put into words how gorgeous you are." I do a little turn so he can get the full effect. "Come here, I think I need a closer inspection to figure out the right word."

"You better stop. We can't keep Paul waiting."

He levels his eyes at me. "Respectfully, fuck Paul."

Then he scoops me over his shoulder, slapping my ass as I laugh and yell for him to put me down. Luis looks thoroughly entertained by us as Rome carries me all the way to my seat. We're presented with a delicious lunch consisting of chips and guacamole, seafood ceviche, and wood grilled chicken and vegetables.

We take our time feeding each other and enjoying the cocktails that were made for us before jumping in the water. After, Rome has me help him set up the Kindle app on his phone so he can continue reading the A.R. Washington book, and I can start a new e-book on our way back to shore.

Days like today stay with you forever and when the dust of mine and Rome's relationship settles, I'll be grateful to have had this.

When we get back to the hotel, Rome immediately passes out. Because I'm not tired at all, I let him keep sleeping peacefully. I kiss him on his forehead and leave him in my room to go find Evie. She texted me while we were on the boat, but Rome refused to let me acknowledge the outside world. I tell her to meet me by the entrance, and we agree to ride bikes into town to do some shopping.

"What did you do with your day of rest?"

I look down at the ground to hide the smile threatening to take over my entire face. "Exactly that, rested. I finished the second A.R. Washington book."

"Oh, that's good. Was the book good?"

"It was the best reading experience I've had in a long time," I say, biting my lip.

"Oop. Okay, girl. Tell me no more about your one-handed reading."

I roll my eyes, going back to rifle through the hangers of shirts in the clothing store we're checking out. "And what did you do with your day miss ma'am?"

"I spent most of the day going back and forth between my pool and my bed. I had planned to go out and find me a little boo ting, but I was too damn tired. Those drinks last night were potent. Is this what we're to look forward to in our thirties? Actual hangovers? I rebuke this."

I didn't feel hungover at all when I woke up today, but then again, I'm pretty sure Rome and I sweat all the alcohol out. "We are in our thirties, Evie."

"No. We're thirty. Next year, we'll be in our thirties. There's a difference."

"Whatever you say."

We look through a few more stores, mostly browsing, but we do get a few pieces of jewelry and handbags. We go into a store that features all types of handmade art. While Evie is looking at the alebrijes, the clay art catches my eye. One in particular, a pair of handcrafted clay sea turtles, makes me think of Rome. Two souls drifting together despite their very nature to be alone. I look around to see if there are any clay giraffes lying around but there aren't.

Decision made. He gave me a memorable day; I want to get him a physical representation of what it meant to me.

"I'm finished. Did you wanna get something?" Evie asks, joining me in front of the clay art.

"Yeah, I think I do."

CHAPTER SIX

Rome

A SWITCH FLIPPED IN THE DAYS AFTER OUR BOAT TRIP. BEFORE, WE were moving with barely put together restraint. We enjoyed each other at night and acted like strangers during the day. But now? She's still holding on to the foolish notion that what we're doing will come to an end after the week is up tomorrow, but in the meantime, she's finally allowing herself to be with me completely, in and out of the bedroom. Every free moment she has is spent with me. She doesn't hesitate to be in my presence around our friends and even though she doesn't allow herself to be affectionate with me, the way we've been outwardly eye fucking each other is bound to get us caught.

I meant what I told her the other day, I'm not afraid of getting caught. I'm drawn to her in a way that I can't explain but I know I need more. Whatever more entails, I want it.

The craving I have for her has me texting her to join me in the gym, even though I just left her not one hour ago.

> Me: Get outta bed and come work out with me

I wipe the sweat already pooled on my forehead with my towel while I wait for her response. The hotel gym is completely empty right now, and normally I would revel in this time to put my headphones in and lose myself in my workout, but J has my mind too gone to be able to do that.

> J: Oh so you think you can just make demands of me now?

> Me: You right that was wild of me. You should come to the gym and set me straight

J: Lol if I were a fool that might have worked

Me: You're a lot of things J but a fool isn't one of em

Me: Come see me

J: Still waiting on my please

Me: I'm not above begging when it comes to you so PLEASE bring your fine ass to the gym I need a workout partner

J: What makes you think I even have workout clothes with me?

Me: Play with ya mama not me

J: How I'm playing?

Me: Bc you know if you didn't have any I'd have some to you within the next thirty minutes so again I say stop playing

J: I see so this was just a chance to flaunt your wealth

Me: No it's me telling you plainly I'll get you whatever you want and need whenever you want and need it

A few minutes go by without a response, so I send a follow up.

Me: Don't take too long processing what I said, J. It's not complicated. I'll see you soon.

J: I didn't agree

Me: Didn't you?

With a smile tugging at my lips, I put my phone down and get back to the goblet squats I was doing. I don't think I can make demands of Janelle, but I know that I'm not alone in this craving. She can chalk it up to wanting to make the most of our limited time together whereas I err more on the side of not being able to get enough of her, but the result is the same: when one of us calls, the other answers.

After my last set, I sit down on the weight bench beside me for a quick rest. The door to the gym opens and I know without looking that it's her. The air in the room shifts, making room for the sheer magnitude of emotions that flow when the two of us are together.

I turn around to take her in and find her watching me with a loosely veiled desire. She looked like a walking fantasy with her ample ass barely covered in some short black biker shorts, paired with a yellow sports bra and black training gloves. The woman had her own training gloves with her but was playing on my phone about not having any workout clothes.

She walks toward me with the confidence of a queen, knowing she has me wrapped around her finger and salivating at the sight of her.

"Couldn't get through a couple hours without me?" She teases, stepping between my legs and bracing her hands on my shoulders. I reach up to grab her chin and pull her face down to mine, losing myself in the pillowy clouds of her lips. She pulls away from me looking breathless and a little dazed but gathers herself to throw another taunt at me. "I thought I came here to work out, but I didn't need to throw on these clothes or drag myself out of bed for this kind of workout."

I grip her hips and stand to my full height. With a slap on her ass, I move past her. "Bring your ass on."

She chuckles but follows me without question.

I let her warm up while I do some leg extensions. I'm obvious in my ogling of her but I don't care. Janelle is a work of art, and she deserves to be appreciated, studied for hours on end. She has the face of an angel and the body of a vixen. I appreciate every curve, dip, and dimple on her.

The way her ass claps on its own with every squat has me about to brick up right here in this gym. She moves through each rep with a grace that showcases the true strength her body possesses.

After her warmups, we talk as we run through different exercises. I like to have fun at the gym. I never take myself too seriously so I tease her during our entire workout, and she gives it right back to me. I make a show out of spotting her during certain exercises so that I can have excuses to touch her. She gives me shit for the bulgarian split squats I put her through, telling me if I wanted to kill her there are more humane ways to do it.

We've now been working out for a solid two hours and I'm ready to go back to one of our rooms to work something else out. I'm sitting on the mat against one of the plyo boxes with one of the free weights straddling my hips, about to do a few sets of hip thrusts before calling it a day when Janelle calls for my attention.

"You tired, old man?"

"Why you say that?"

"Them weights looking a little light. I'm just surprised is all."

Oh, she has jokes. I have two hundred pounds of weights on this bar and she's looking like I'm lifting a sandwich. "Word? Okay. How much you think I should add?"

She shrugs noncommittally. "You could do three. Three fifty."

"Bet." This was supposed to be my cool down, but now I've got other ideas.

Her eyes balk at my concession. "I was just fucking with you, Rome. Do your damn workout."

"I am. Come here."

"Nah."

"J. Come here."

I hear her mumble *shit* under her breath before she makes her way over to me with a sheen of sweat covering her body.

"Put your legs here," I pat the spots on both sides of me and she tilts her head in confusion.

"Why would I do that?"

"Because I want you to get on top. That's gonna get me to that three you wanted so bad."

She laughs humorlessly. "Hell no."

"Something wrong?"

She looks at me as though she may have to get me checked out by a professional before narrowing her eyes. "It's cute that you think me getting on top would get you to three. Fucking with me is gonna put you over four hundred pounds. You sure you wanna do this?"

My face remains flat because does she think I'm some kind of punk? "Do I look unsure?"

"No. You look very confident."

"Okay then."

She closes her eyes and lets out a resigned sigh. "You better not drop me, Rome Anthony Martin."

"You don't ever have to worry about me letting you fall, Janelle Lashaun Cross. Now sit."

She steps over the bar and carefully lowers herself onto the center as she pierces my soul with her eyes.

Gripping the bar tightly I settle into position and begin my reps. The sounds of my harsh grunts fill the room as I move through the first ten reps. Janelle's hands are braced against my chest but she's silent. I expect her to be nervous, worried about me dropping her but instead she's looking at me with complete trust. Her bottom lip is trapped between her teeth and her hooded lids tell me where her thoughts have gone.

I take a brief rest after the first ten, taking a minute to lean in and kiss her. "Told you this was lightwork, J."

"You know, this is a lesson I'm happy to learn. You got another set in you?"

I laugh and thrust my hips up to begin the next set, cutting off any retorts from her. When I finish the second set, she scoots backward a little so that her ass hangs off the bar a little and she grips her arms onto my shoulders. I can practically feel her pussy clenching for me, and I know I have about five minutes to be inside of her before we both lose our minds.

"Please tell me that was the last set," she murmurs.

"You tapping out on me?"

"I'm tapping in. I think we both could use a shower, don't you?" Say no more.

Once Janelle and I have spent a thorough amount of time in the shower, I reluctantly let her go to start her day. Amerie had been blowing up her phone while we were in the gym, so she needed to go find her. The ladies have a cooking class tonight as well, so I'm not expecting to see her again until after that.

Christian and Micah hit me up to grab lunch at one of the hotel bars, so I head down and find them both there already.

"What's good, y'all?" I touch fists with them both before grabbing a seat at the barstool two seats down from Micah. The place is pretty much empty, so we have the space to spread out and give ourselves the leg room needed without interfering with other guests.

"Yo. I feel like I haven't seen y'all this whole trip," Christian says.

He isn't wrong. Christian, Micah, and Arnold are my boys, but we don't feel the need to be up each other's asses all the time. There are group activities planned for every single day once the wedding guests arrive, so we're using this time to enjoy some peace and quiet with paradise as our backdrop while Amerie is using this time to force her sister and friends into doing her bidding under the guise of bonding.

"You've been diving into any and every pussy as always and Rome's been doing whatever he's been doing," Micah gave me a pointed look with that statement.

"We've been here, what? Six days? And I've only slept with three women, so I don't think that counts as any and every," Christian quips, clearly proud of himself.

Micah shakes his head with laughter. "You don't have a lick of sense. Acting like your dick's gonna fall off if you don't slide up in something every damn day."

"Aye, bruh. Don't knock me because I got a healthy libido."

"Yeah aight. You keep letting your dick run your life, you gon be the one who ends up fucked."

Christian's jaw drops at that and I burst out laughing. "Ayooo, I'm not even gonna respond to that."

"Nothing you can say really," Micah shrugs.

I don't even know why Christian is surprised at this point. Micah has always gotten on Christian for his 'there's plenty for everyone' ways ever since we met in college. We're just lucky that he's not dumb on top of having no taste, or else he'd probably have more children than Nick Cannon.

"Man, anyway, what have **you** been up to this week, Micah?"

"I've been working."

"Working? The fuck? Nah, you know what? That tracks."

"Exactly. Act like you know me."

Micah is an artist, a painter specifically, specializing in the realistic art style. His stuff is dope as hell. He's painted portraits for several celebrities and politicians which has made him a household name. He now owns a gallery back home that only features Black artists, giving them the platform needed to kick off their careers. He picked up photography as a hobby because he wanted to be able to go home and paint the things and people he saw while traveling. He could afford to have some kind of traveling studio so that he could bring his art wherever he went, but he wouldn't spend that kind of money on himself. Only his parents and younger sister would get him to spend the big bucks, and they would never even ask for it. If he says he's been working all week, I'm sure he and his camera have been going hard.

"Where's Arnold?" I ask, knowing he can't be with Amerie because she's with Janelle.

"Getting some business calls done while Amerie's busy and can't get on his ass," Christian offers.

The bartender brings out our food and Christian can't help but to flirt with her as she fills more drink orders for the waiting servers. When he gets up to go to the bathroom, Micah turns to me.

"So, you've been busy this week with a certain Cross sister."

"Since when are you into tea? That's more Christian and Arnold's lane."

He holds up his hands in surrender. "I'm just wondering how much longer I gotta keep running interference for you every time somebody comes looking for you or her."

The day I took Janelle out on the boat, he was the one who kept everyone occupied so no one would notice both of us were gone and several times he stopped Amerie from coming to Janelle's room looking for her.

"Per our arrangement, this is over as of tomorrow night."

He hits me with an incredulous look. "And you believe that?"

"Hell no. I spent a lot of time running from Janelle. I'm not about to do it again so this next week is about to be an interesting ride."

"Well shit, let me get ready for the storm."

A little while later, I'm walking to my room and I see Janelle walking toward me. A wide smile graces her face and I swear I'd spend my life trying to keep it there.

That thought knocks me back a step but it stays there, taking root in my mind.

"Fancy meeting you here."

I look behind her and then pin her to the wall, leaning so I'm hovering over her with my hand resting above her head.

"Were you coming from my room?"

"I may have been looking for you."

"You found me. I thought you were busy today."

"I was and am. But I had some free time and I..." she cuts herself off.

"You what, Janelle?"

"I just wanted to stop by."

"If you missed me, let me know something, J. Don't let me be alone in the shit."

"Aww, you missed me?"

"What I tell you about the games you play?"

She places her hand against my chest, drumming her finger up and down my chest. "Okay, okay. I missed you and wanted to say hi. Better?"

"Much. How much free time you got?"

"Hmm well I..."

"Yo, Romey-Rome!" Her words are cut off by Arnold's voice behind me.

She drops her hand to her side, but I don't rush to move from my position. Number one, I don't want to and two, it would look more suspicious if I jumped away.

"What's up Arnold?"

He daps me up when he reaches me but furrows his brow at Janelle. "Hey, Janelle. I didn't see you there."

"What's up, Arnold?" She mirrors my greeting.

"What y'all up to?"

"I just ran into Rome on my way to my next task, so we were catching up."

"Oh okay. Well, speaking of tasks, Rome I need a big favor."

"What's up?"

"I was supposed to go to this shop in town to pick up these candles Ri wanted for the ceremony days ago, but I forgot. She wants to see them and approve them today, but if she sees me leave to go get them at this point I'm a dead man. Could you please go pick 'em up for me?"

"I mean, yeah I can, but how am I gonna get 'em to you without her seeing?"

"I can just bring her with me to your room to pick 'em up. I'll tell her I gave them to you to hold onto."

"Bet. I'll go right now."

"It's you plotting to lie to my sister in front of me for me," Janelle mocks with a gleam in her eye.

He has the sense to look chastised. "Come on, Janelle. You know your sister. I don't wanna ruin any of this for her."

Spoken just like Janelle. Everyone seems to tiptoe around Amerie and that irks me.

"My lips are sealed."

"I appreciate that," he slaps my hand with his, pulling me into an embrace. "Thanks Rome, I'm just praying they have what she wanted because she wasn't able to order ahead so we're at the mercy of what the shop has in stock. Now I just gotta keep her distracted 'til you get back. It shouldn't be too hard, or maybe it should." He laughs at his own joke and then turns to look at Janelle with remorse. "Sorry, Janelle…I…"

She holds up her hand to stop him. "Arnold, please. Get over yourself," she turns back to me. "Actually, can I go with you? I need to go to town anyway."

"Of course."

Arnold looks between us with an unreadable expression before he nods and heads back in the direction he came.

Janelle waits until he turns the corner to let the corners of her mouth tip up again. "Guess you got me for a little bit longer then."

Exactly how I want it.

We head to the concierge desk to pick up two bikes and then make our way to town.

The streets of Tulum are paved with palm trees and fairy lights. The cars are bumper to bumper so I'm glad we opted for bikes instead of driving. We pass by several storefronts selling things from oranges to clothes to scooters.

Once we get to an empty stretch of sidewalk, I pick up the pace to ride alongside Janelle instead of behind her.

She reaches her left hand out to me, keeping a tight grip on the handlebar with her right. I match her and take her hand in mine. We ride in silence with our hands intertwined for three blocks before we come up on a mother and son walking down the street and need to separate.

I get her to pull over with me because I need to grab my phone and look up the place Arnold sent me. We stop at a stand selling guava and some other fruit.

"I think my legs are about to fall off," Janelle says, bending over at the waist and grabbing her knees.

"J, are you okay?"

"Yeah, I'm good. If *someone* hadn't tried to kill me earlier with fucking bulgarian split squats, I'd be a lot better."

"Ah, we back to that, huh?" I drop to a squat, rubbing my hands along her legs.

Her eyes drift close. "We never left that. Who the hell voluntarily does bulgarian split squats?"

I shrug and stand to my full height, hovering over her. "Me?"

"I'm never working out with you again."

"You gonna act like you didn't like our workout?"

She peers up at me through her curvy lashes. Her lips fall open slightly. "I mean I didn't say all of it."

Not wanting to resist anymore, I lean down and kiss her.

"Disculpe," one of the men working at the fruit stand interrupts. Janelle tucks her head against my chest in embarrassment before looking at him. "Fruta?" He asks.

"Oh, um, well," she walks over to the line of fruit, observing the guava but taking an interest in the fruit next to it. "Um. Oh shit, how do you say it? Que es eso?" She asks, pointing to the fruit.

He tells her it's a tuna fruit and rather than trying to explain further he simply grabs a pair of gloves and one of the fruits. He grabs a knife from his cart and slices the ends off the fruit then carefully peels back the skin. He slices a piece and hands it to her and she eats it in one bite.

Moaning around it, she looks at me with wide eyes. "This is so good!"

The man behind the cart looks pleased and offers her another piece which she shares with me.

"Quieres comprar uno?"

"Should we get some?"

"Is that what you want?"

She wrinkles her nose and looks carefully at the fruit. "Yeah, it is."

"Then it's yours."

She tilts her head from side to side and then bows her head. When she pulls her backpack around to her front and pulls out her wallet, I put my hand on her wrist. "Janelle. Don't insult me."

"I can pay for some fruit, Rome."

"I know you can, but when you're in my presence you should never be reaching for your wallet."

"I give you one romance book and you don't know how to act."

I smirk and put her backpack back on her shoulders. "I would never take pointers from Jharrel's corny ass. But you wait 'til I get my hands on book two. You done fucked up now."

I give the man the seventy-four pesos he asks for in exchange for a bundle of the tuna fruit and put it in Janelle's basket.

When we get to the candle store, we're inundated with candles in all different styles and colors. Some are shaped like tea kettles and mugs. Others are shaped like basins, trinkets, and even faces. An overpowering scent of vanilla fills the space, canceling out all the scents from the different pieces.

We are welcomed in the store by a woman named Luz who tells us all about how the candles are all handmade and how most of them have herbs or crystals within them.

Janelle asks Luz for the candle we're looking for and thankfully she does have them, but she only has three so hopefully Amerie will be satisfied with that.

Luz must help another customer before she can pack up our order, so we scan the remaining rows of candles.

Janelle picks up a navy blue and white candle that is shaped like a teapot, inspecting it closely. "You know what I was thinking?"

My brows pique at her question. "What?"

"I was thinking that I could expand Labor of Love to be more than just a birthing center." When she first told me about her plans for Labor of Love over a year ago, I told her it was a brilliant idea. We've talked about it a few times on this trip as well and I'm happy to see she's still just as passionate about it.

"Okay, expand how?"

She gets a faraway look in her eye. I'm not even sure if she's really talking to me or if she's in her head. Either way, I'm enraptured with what she has to say. "You remember at first, I just wanted it to be a birth center geared toward women of color, specifically Black women. The mortality rate for Black women during childbirth is three times higher than that of white women, so it was important to me to offer them alternative approaches to hospital births with doctors who look like them and not only hear them but listen to them. That's still my goal, of course, but I just keep thinking there's more that can be done. The care of Black women is sorely lacking in several areas, not just childbirth. I'd like to offer other services too. Mental health services, counseling, holistic medicine, homeopathy, nutrition and dietary counseling. I want it to be a one stop shop for Black women, make all their care easily accessible with doctors they can trust."

I smile at the excitement in her voice. Her energy feeds me in a way I've never felt before. Her drive to serve her community drives me to keep striving to do my part for our city.

"That's a great idea. Where are you with your planning now?"

"I've been toying with the idea of expanding the center to be Labor of Love Health Center rather than Labor of Love Birth Center for a while, but something about these crystals and herbs embedded in these candles got me thinking about it again."

"Take it as your sign, then."

"Yeah. If I do it, I would need to form a board of doctors to invest and help me with it. I was prepared to go into it alone when it was just a birth center because I already have a network of doulas and midwives who would come work with me. I don't have the network for the other services though."

"Yet."

She stands up straighter. "Yet. You're right." She looks at me with a shy smile. "I already found a place I like for it. I haven't looked it up in a minute so it could be off the market by now but it's perfect."

"Where is it?"

She rattles off the location and I have to fight to keep the emotions off my face. The location she wants for her health center is a building I already own.

I had originally bought it with the intention of doing something with it for The Baltimore Collective but given the fact that it used to be some kind of clinic before it shut down, it would be an ideal setting for Labor of Love.

The Baltimore Collective is a foundation that Arnold, Christian, Micah, and I started because we wanted to see to the growth of our city. We offer scholarships for minority students in our fields of study—computer science, sports management, communications or journalism, and art. We also offer mentor programs for all minority students whether they want to pursue a college degree or not.

We've all bought buildings in and around the city to use for businesses made for us, by us. If my building is the location Janelle wants for her center, I'll hand her the keys tomorrow. Getting her to agree to that, however, would be impossible. I'll let her go about it in her own way. In the meantime, I make a mental note to put together a list of contractors I can give her that can help get the building where it needs to be.

"That's a great location. It sounds like you got it all figured out. You just need to go for it."

She sets the candle she was holding back on the shelf, tapping her lip with her finger. "Yeah, maybe. If the building is still available, then I'll commit to looking for doctors who can join the mission." She rears back at the Cheshire grin clouding my face. "Why do you look like that?"

"Nothing, I just have a feeling this is all going to work out in your favor."

"I guess we'll see, won't we?"

"I guess so."

When Luz brings out our package, we carefully put them in the basket on Janelle's bike and make our way back to the hotel.

We continue talking about her ideas for Labor of Love until it's time for her to head to her cooking class, leaving me with nothing to do. I download the second book in the series she put me onto and dive in.

Me: My room tonight?

The bubbles start and stop on my screen several times for quite a few minutes before a reply finally comes through.

J: I'm struggling

Me: With what?

> J: I want to tell you no that I'm staying in my own room by myself tonight bc it's been a shitty night and I'm in a bad mood

> Me: So what's the struggle?

> J: I don't want you to suffer my attitude but I know you're the only one who can make me feel less shitty and I promised you my yes's

I hate that she had a terrible night, no doubt a result of whatever bullshit Amerie must've been on tonight, but I do love that she knows I can make it better. Even if she's trying to fight it.

> Me: Doesn't seem like a struggle at all then. Come to my room. Let me take care of you

I don't receive an answer to my text. Instead, I get a soft knock on my door five minutes later. I open it to find Janelle looking beautiful as always in black wide leg pants and a pink, white, and black floral embroidered crop top. Her hair is pulled back into an intricate ponytail with a pink headpiece adorning her head like a crown. She looks exquisite but the one thing missing from her attire is her confidence. She's practically hunched over with her eyes firmly planted on the ground, no trace of the bold woman I'm quickly becoming addicted to.

I pull her inside and kiss her temple. Her eyes squeeze shut upon contact. "Want to tell me about it?"

"I- I think she hates me," she whispers then jumps, shocked to hear the words come out of her own mouth.

"Amerie?" I hold out a bottle of water to her and she absentmindedly takes a sip.

"All night—all night she just kept throwing digs at me. About every fucking thing. My cooking, my outfit, my career, my love life. It was nonstop. Dani even got in her ass about it, and you know she's normally on some keep the peace shit with us. What did I do?"

"You didn't do anything, J."

"No. I must've done something because this isn't us. This passive aggressive hostility. It's not how we operate, and I am trying to understand where the fuck we went wrong."

I plant my hands at the base of her neck to keep her from going too far into her head. "Tell me what you need right now."

"Honestly? I wanna beat her ass. I think that might make me feel better right now," she sighs. "But I know I'll feel like shit about it in the morning. Maybe I should leave."

"Leave Tulum?"

"Yeah. Maybe she should make Dani the Maid of Honor and I should just go home."

"And you wouldn't feel like shit leaving before your sister's wedding? Come on, J. You know yourself better than that."

"I don't know what else to do. I am losing my sister and I don't know how to make it stop."

"So lose her."

Her neck snaps back and she glares at me. "What?"

"Sometimes the people who are supposed to love you the most are the ones who hurt you the worst. They don't get a pass just because they're family. Choose yourself." I've seen the damage holding onto a toxic relationship of any kind can cause and I don't want that for her.

She takes a moment to mull that over and I want her to think very carefully about it. Arnold is my boy and I respect he and Amerie's relationship but what I won't do is tolerate disrespect shown to Janelle. She has become far too important to me for me to watch her lose herself trying to save a relationship that isn't serving her.

"I don't want to give up on my sister."

I can't make her cut off her sister. All I can do is be there for her through this and hope that eventually she sees the people who are worth her time and the ones who aren't. "Then allow me to take away the pain tonight."

She looks at me with glossy eyes and dips her head bashfully. I pull her into me and kiss her with everything in me. I want her to feel this kiss down to her toes. I want what I feel for her to be imprinted on her skin. I grip the waistband of her pants and pull them down, dropping to my knees so I can provide her with support to get her shoes and pants off. She looks down at me with pure adoration and it hits me so deeply in the chest I almost fall over.

When I stand back up, she helps me get her top off, leaving her in nothing but her pink lace lingerie set. I back her up to the bed, picking her up and placing her right in the middle.

"I want to try something with you. Do you trust me?"

"Yes," she says without hesitation.

I grab the edge wrap scarf I bought for her in case she found herself in my room without it and place it on the bed. Then, I go to the bathroom and take the belts from the robes the hotel provided and add them to the pile.

Taking a moment to appreciate the sight of her on the bed, nipples pebbled through her bra, legs spread, and face tinged with curiosity, I rummage through my carryon to find my headphones and add them to the pile on the bed.

I sit on the edge of the bed, keeping my feet on the floor. "I want to explain to you exactly what I want to do so you're not afraid."

"Okay."

"I want to take away your senses one by one. I think right now what you're struggling with is the need to control the outcome of what happens between you and your sister. You said you like the freedom of having to give away control sometimes, so I'd like to show you the pleasure you can experience by surrendering control elsewhere."

"Have you done this before?"

"I have." While I'm not a pro by any means, I feel comfortable enough that I can give her what she needs, safely.

"What will you do?"

"You can play around with one sense or all of them. For tonight, I'd like to focus on three: touch, sight, and hearing." I go into detail about how I will use the headphones, scarf, and robe ties and she eyes the items on the bed as I do. "If it ever gets to be too much, you tell me and I'll stop. Okay?"

"I'm with you."

I lean down to suck her nipple to my mouth through her bra. Her hands immediately fly to the back of my neck as I undo the clasps of her bra. When the final clasp is undone, I release her nipple so that I can slide the bra down her arms.

She lifts her hips so I can pull her panties down, her folds already glistening with her desire for me. Grabbing the robe ties, I grab one of her wrists and bind it to the bedpost. I do the same with the other wrist and then I double check to make sure both ties are flat so as not to cut off her circulation and that neither are tied too tight. She pulls against the restraints, seemingly pleased with the level of resistance.

"I don't have enough to bind your feet so I'm going to leave them free. I'm trusting you to not use them to touch me, J. Can you be my good girl and do that for me?"

Her eyes darken as she licks her lips. "You can trust me."

A sinister smile creeps up on my face. "Good." I trace light circles around her inner thigh and she squirms under my touch. So sensitive already. I cover her entire body with gentle touches. Soft foot massages, a swipe of my fingers across her nipples, a chaste kiss against her belly. Her movements become more erratic. With every caress, she bucks beneath my fingers, but not in an effort to push me away. No, she's trying to pull me in closer. Make me as desperate for her as she feels at this moment. Little does she know, my desperation for her is a constant that I've grown accustomed to quite quickly.

I want to disabuse her of the notion that instant gratification is the name of the game tonight. Tonight is all about letting go.

"Rome, please. I need you," she cries, trying like hell to keep her legs pinned to the bed but failing.

"Do you not like the way I touch you, J?" My fingers spread her pussy, causing her eyes to slam shut.

"Mmm, I want more," she moans.

Seeing her like this; delirious with want when I've barely touched her brings out an animalistic pride in me. The kind that makes you want to beat your chest and claim her to the world.

I reach behind me for the scarf and hold it out in front of her. "You ready for this?"

She nods her head insistently. "I'm so ready."

I tie the scarf around her eyes, not too tight but tight enough so I know it won't slip. "Can you see me?"

"N-no."

"Good. Relax, J. I got you."

I stand from the bed, and she notices the shift of weight on the bed immediately. Her head jerks to the now empty space. Quietly, I move to the foot of the bed so I can watch her. Her legs flail around, trying to create the friction she craves but failing to add up to what I can provide. She starts to tug at her restraints whipping her head from side to side in hopes to hear the slightest movement from me.

I grab one of the pillows from the couch which has fringe tassels on the bottom and walk ever so slowly over to the left side of the bed.

Leaning forward I whisper in her ear. "You look like pure sin laying before me right now." Her only response is a deep moan, pulled from the depths of her diaphragm. I hold one of the tassels from the pillow to her skin and swirl it around her neck.

"Oh fuck."

I drag the tassel down her body, drawing different patterns in different places on her skin. I take pauses at random moments so she can't anticipate my next move.

"I want to touch you," she whimpers.

"I know you do, but you know you can't. Right?"

"Yessss."

"I love when you give me your yes's so freely." She clenches her thighs at that. Done taking things lightly, I toss the pillow aside and straddle her hips. "I want you to see me worship your body, J. Worship you." Her forehead creases and even through the scarf I can see her eyebrows pique. "Not with your eyes, J. I want you to really see me." I whisper in her ear. "Feel me. Can you do that for me?"

"Yes!"

I suck her earlobe into my mouth and lick a trail along the outer shell until she bucks her hips, trying to make contact with my already achingly hard dick.

I move to her other ear to whisper, "You are a dream come true."

My tongue finds the nape of her neck and charts a path down the column of her throat to the base. "You are exquisitely beautiful."

I kiss the top of her sternum. "You give so much of yourself to others." A kiss to the top of her breast. "You deserve to have that reciprocated."

Her teeth sink into her bottom lip as she groans. "Rome."

I swirl my tongue around her nipple, laving it thoroughly before I bite down on it, eliciting a wild moan from her. "You are deserving of a love that embellishes your brilliance." Deep in my gut I have a feeling that Amerie is intimidated by Janelle and everything she brings to the table, so she'd rather diminish it than nurture its growth. I don't want to diminish her. I want to stand back and watch her shine.

I move to her other nipple and glide my hand up to tweak this one. "You are an amazing sister. Daughter. Friend. Doctor. Those who meet you are lucky to know you."

I slide my body down her legs, trailing my tongue down the path of her stomach. "You deserve all the success you've accomplished already and all the success that's yet to come." Her body is practically vibrating with need.

A kiss to her lower belly.

"Rome, what are you doing to me?"

"Do you want me to stop?"

"Never."

The word settles over me like a cloak, blanketing me in its finality. Before I take away her last sense, I want her to hear the pleasure it gives me to please her.

"Mmmm," she cries out as my tongue plunges into her. I devour her, using my nose as the pressure point on her clit. My hands seek out the sensitive parts of her body. I find her hip bone and lower back, not giving her a moment to prepare before I start tickling her.

Her body convulses with unexpected laughter then dissolves into mewls and whimpers and back to laughter.

"Oh shit, what the fuck?"

"Mhm, I like the way your pussy grips me when you laugh, J. I want you to come just like that."

She hisses from the pleasurable pain of me biting her inner thigh, twisting her arms in her restraints to no avail.

"Let me hear you."

She delivers a lethal combination of a scream, moan, and laugh when I latch on to her clit at the same time that I dig into her ticklish spots. The sound bounces off the walls, shaking the room. I don't come up for air until I'm drowning in her release, feeling every bone in her body pulsate around me.

"You did so good, J. So good. How do you feel?"

"I feel incredible," she says, her voice hoarse.

"Do you need a break?"

She shakes her head passionately, fighting to keep her legs flat on the bed but a full body shiver hits her when she accidentally crosses one leg over the other.

"No. More," she begs.

Reaching over to pick up my headphones, I turn on a playlist on my phone and hold them up to Janelle. "Remember you won't be able to hear me but I can hear you so if you need me to stop, tell me."

"Mhmm," she mewls.

Placing the headphones squarely over her ears, she's plunged into complete quiet and darkness. It can be scary to be in that kind of environment for too long when you're not used to it, so I don't waste any time throwing her legs over my shoulders and thrusting inside of her. I want my body to serve as her anchor, tethering her to this moment here with me.

With the music taking away her ability to know how loud she's being, her screams are even more intense. Her inhibitions melt away, not worried about anything but feeling. I push her legs down under my arms and lean forward, hitting the spot I know drives her wild.

I switch my pace up a few times so that she can't try to match my rhythm, giving her no choice but to let me lead the dance we're tangled in. The slow strokes grant me the low groans that she pulls from somewhere deep in her belly. The fast strokes earn me the soprano screams that scratch her vocal cords. Together they make a beautiful song for my ears only. I could listen to the symphony of her all day.

I can feel her walls start to tighten and her legs begin to shake so I know my time is running out. She'll need a break after this round so with the freedom of being the only one in the room able to hear my words, I speak a truth that has demands to be released.

"I could see myself falling in love with you, Janelle," I groan out her name as her orgasm triggers mine, sending us crashing to the ground.

Yanking the headphones off her, I rush to get the rest of the bindings off her. Her eyes are squeezed shut when I take off the scarf, fluttering open ever so slowly to readjust to the light. I scan her wrists for any signs of irritation or bruising but they appear to be okay, so I kiss both of them, massaging them lightly.

"That was…" she stutters. She flops back down on the bed, not even attempting to find the word she was looking for a moment ago.

I let her sleep for a minute while I go run a bath for us. I use cool water to soothe her muscles and joints, and then I guide her into the bath, sitting her in front of me so she can lean on me for support while I bathe her.

After I clean her body, I hold her in my arms, brushing my forehead against the top of her spine. We stay there until our teeth start to chatter, telling us it's time to get out.

She sidles up to me in bed, not wanting an inch of space between us and I'm all too happy to oblige. Grabbing my phone, I download a book of her choice and read to her until her soft snores fill the room.

CHAPTER SEVEN

Janelle

I T'S THE END OF THE WEEK.

Tomorrow our families and friends will start arriving and Rome and I will cease to exist.

Everything in me wants me to extend our time together. Every cell in my body wants to latch on to him and never let go, but that's just not a possibility. We work so well together because we've managed to exist outside of the planes of reality—Outside of familial influence, responsibilities, and expectations. When all of that comes crashing down around us, I don't think we'll survive. My soul feels like I know him on a deeper level than I've ever known anyone, but how can that be possible in such a short amount of time?

It isn't. So, it's best to just end while the memory of him still lights me up with joy.

Today, we have a group activity on our itineraries but it's one that fills me with excitement rather than dread. We're swimming with sea turtles!

When Ri let me know that she didn't have a sea turtle excursion anywhere on the agenda for our time in Tulum, I was disappointed, but I didn't want to make the trip about me so I kept quiet. Resigned to the idea that I would do it by myself if I could find the free time, but then she texted us to let us know that we were doing that instead of the errands she had planned for the day.

If this is her idea of an olive branch, I appreciate it wholeheartedly.

Our guides get us set up with snorkeling gear and go through a safety lesson with us before loading us onto the boat that will take us out onto Akumal Bay.

The water is a serene turquoise color. The wind against the waves gives a refreshing chill to the otherwise humid air.

Rome, Micah, myself, and Dani are the first to dive into the water. As our guide is helping Dani with her vest, Rome sends me a sly smile. He knows how much this moment means to me and the pure elation on his face from the fact that I get to experience it brings a tear to my eye. I jump in the water and let it wash away with the waves.

Once we dip below the surface, I am bombarded by the beauty of this underwater world. When surrounded by the expanse of the sea, you realize just how small you really are.

Feeling a little overwhelmed, I swim back up to the surface. The snorkeling aspect is a little hard to adjust to at first. Even though I know I'm breathing, it feels like I'm not and it sends a minor panic through me.

"J, I found one." In the middle of the sea, I can hear his voice loud and clear like it's only meant for me to hear.

I turn to see him with his hand out to me and fuck if I don't want to pull him to me and lose myself despite the audience. He seems to sense my thoughts and gives me a saccharine smile. I grab his hand and let him pull me under all to come face to face with a beautiful sea turtle. Our guide swims over, but we don't disconnect our hands until Dani and Micah find their way over to us. Evie, Arnold, Ri, and Christian join us in the water and when the guide pulls out a container of food, more sea turtles surround us.

One of them looks like it's trying to bite our guide, but he simply grabs it by its front fin and pushes it upward. The little guy completely changes its trajectory and moves on somewhere else.

I forget all about my trouble with snorkeling and am the last one to swim to the surface for a break. Eventually, the others grow tired of snorkeling and opt to stay on the boat, whereas Rome and I continue to go under and soak it all in. These marvelous creatures have allowed us into their space, and I want to make the most of it while I can. This is absolutely breathtaking.

After the tour, I am so worn out I can barely keep my head up on the boat ride back. It's something I'll never forget though and it makes me glad I didn't leave like I threatened to last night.

When we get back to shore, the group takes off for the beach and I step back to give myself one more moment to admire the water. A shadow falls over me and I tilt my head back to see Micah smiling down at me. "Did you have fun?" he asks.

"I had the time of my life. Sea turtles are my favorite favorite."

Micah hangs his head as if I've just told the funniest joke in the world. "That makes sense then."

"What does?"

"Nothing, my fault. I'm all over the place."

It's obvious he's lying but I just don't know why. Maybe I'm not the only one in this wedding party with secrets.

"Well, did you have fun?" I return the question back to him.

"Oh yeah, it was dope. I liked that it was just us too. Rome did his thing."

My head seemingly detaches from my body with how fast it flies back to look at Micah. "Rome?"

My question seems to spark a few of his own and he cycles through them internally before a look of peace takes over his face, and I know whatever decision he's made is about to punch me in the gut.

"Yeah, Rome's the one who set this whole tour up, said he heard about it from a local and thought everyone would enjoy it. He wouldn't even hear it when Arnold told him we didn't have time to make it happen. He said he was booking it and whoever could make time was welcome to come."

"Is that right?"

"Yep. Seemed really important to him."

This whole time I thought that because Ri was the one who texted me about it that she was the one who set it up and that she did it for me when really Rome was once again proving that he gives a fuck.

I have a theory on why Micah decided to share all of this with me, but his answer to my next statement will confirm or deny. "I'm not surprised. Rome's a good guy."

"He is. Probably one of the best. There's one thing you should probably know about him."

"What's that?"

"Once he's decided he wants something? He works relentlessly to get it. And keep it."

And there it is. He knows.

I should be furious at Rome because I was very clear about not wanting our friends to know, but I can't knock him for needing a sounding board for our whole situation. I've wanted to share with Evie since day one, but I let my desire to keep us in the safe bubble away from bullshit outweigh my desire to gush about a man to my friend.

It does feel good to know that Micah approves, if him keeping his mouth shut is any indication. "I'm actually starting to understand that, Micah."

He offers me his arm when my foot sinks too far into the sand and walks with me back to the group. "I've been meaning to tell you, Micah, that Ri showed me the painting you made for her and Arnold for their wedding before we left. It's gorgeous." The painting he created of the two of them is so well done it could be mistaken for a photograph. It's the finer details of the painting that set it apart though. Woven into the minor details of their clothing are things that represent them. There are small footballs, basketballs, baseballs, etc for Arnold. For Ri, there are needles, thread, and sketchpads. But in the center where their hands meet are the things that represent them as a couple. The car from their first road trip together, the plate of spaghetti from their first date, the spot in Patterson Park where he proposed. He captured their journey to each other in the painting, but you would only notice it if you knew where to look.

"Thank you. I'm proud of that one."

"As you should be. I wanted to ask you if you do murals by any chance."

"I definitely could. Why? You got something going on?"

I think about the space back home that I want to create. The vision that Rome helped bring clarity to. "Not yet."

"Well, you say the word and I got you. We're gonna be seeing a lot more of each other so you know I'll take care of you."

My eyes cut to his. "We'll be seeing a lot more of each other?"

"Yeah. Isn't your sister marrying my friend? I imagine that puts us in the same circle."

I bow my head with a smirk. "Oh, right."

The grin he sends my way is slick with mockery. If he weren't so damn handsome, I'd want to slap the grin off him. "Why? Is there another reason we might be seeing a lot more of each other?" He asks, the implication in his voice clear.

I chew on my bottom lip, shaking my head. "I have no idea what you're talking about."

"I bet you don't." He pats my arm as we reach the group and makes his way over to Dani, and for the briefest of moments I see her look at him with what looks like longing before she slips back into a mask of indifference.

I catch Rome's eye and he mouths the words 'you okay' to me to which I wink at him and he smiles.

"If you're horny, let's do it. Ride it, my pony," Evie sings "My Pony" by Ginuwine and dances her way down the aisle while everyone laughs.

"Evie, be fucking forreal," Dani says in between laughs. "That is not what you'd walk down the aisle to."

We're supposed to be having a sort of wedding rehearsal tonight, even though the space won't be decorated until the night before the wedding, followed by a group dinner to celebrate our last night having this place to ourselves. Instead of taking it seriously, however, this has deteriorated into karaoke night with us challenging each other to sing the song we'd want to walk down the aisle to or the song we'd pick for our wives to walk down the aisle to.

"What you mean?" Evie sucks her teeth. "If I find a man that makes me wanna give up my last name, it must mean he's laying down soul snatching peen, and so I will commemorate it appropriately. Y'all will be lucky if we make it to our own reception."

"No, the song fits her because she's probably gonna elope," I point out.

"Even better. Now can I continue my performance? Damn, have some decorum y'all."

She continues singing "My Pony" all the way down the aisle, making sex faces at Micah and gagging faces at Christian. Christian rolls his eyes at her but his song of choice is "I Wanna Sex You Up".

Dani picks "When I See You" by Fantasia and Ri, Evie, and I act as her backup singers.

Micah takes his turn next. "*I believe in you and me. I believe that we will be in love eternally. Well, as far as I can see.*" He continues singing "I Believe in You and Me" by Whitney Houston for a few more lines and when he finishes, we all stand with slack jaws.

"Why y'all looking at me like that?"

"Where the hell have you been hiding that voice?" Evie shrieks.

"I haven't been hiding it."

"The fuck you haven't. I haven't heard you sing so much as Happy Birthday, but you over here busting out Whitney and making her sound like Barry White?" Christian adds.

Micah wipes his hands down the front of his shirt with a coy smirk. "I'm a very right brained individual. Y'all know this."

"So that means you can just sing your ass off? Micah, I'm bout to throw my thong at you right now, stop playing," Evie teases.

"You might sing better than you paint, bro." Christian whistles.

Micah cuts his eyes over to Christian. "Watch ya mouth. I'm an artist and I'm sensitive about my shit," he says as he chucks the deuces up and walks away.

I'm up next and I decide to go with "Have You Ever" by Brandy. When I get to the line about needing something so bad you can't sleep at night, I don't even think Rome realizes that he nods along heavily.

Fuck.

Rome picks "I Gotta Be" by Jagged Edge, which cracks everyone up because he's so into the song he performs the entire damn thing. Christian tries to cut him off but he stiff arms him and keeps going.

Since Ri and Arnold already have their wedding song picked out, they decide to sing "'03 Bonnie and Clyde" together to close us out.

We make our way to the patio where dinner will be held and there is a beautiful buffet display waiting for us. Arnold explains that he had the rehearsal dinner catered by Highly Catered, a private caterer that specializes in THC infused dishes, as an extra treat for us.

Our hostess explains to us that the buffet is loaded with braised oxtail, cajun lobster mac n cheese, jerk lamb chops, shrimp pasta, jollof rice, ackee pasta, and garlic crusted broccoli. She further explains that there are dishes with no THC in them in case anyone doesn't want to participate or wants to eat more later but doesn't want to keep eating the food with THC in it.

Ri asks Arnold to give a toast but he's already making his plate, officially done with hosting us. I can't blame him, the food looks and smells heavenly.

I load my plate up with some of everything, shoveling a big spoonful into my mouth the moment I sit down.

"Look, look, look. They're synchronized," I hear Christian say.

I peek at Dani and Evie, noting that all three of us are doing a happy dance as we eat the mac n cheese.

We all laugh, and I expect Evie to have something smart to say but she's too busy stuffing her face to care what Christian has to say.

I hate to say this, but I think if I'm going to spend long periods of time with Ri for the remainder of this trip, I'm going to have to get her high first.

She's been nothing but a giggling machine since eating and it's the cutest thing. I can do no wrong in her eyes right now, everything I say is the funniest shit she's ever heard. She's just like a baby, so easily pleased.

"I just love pasta so much. I think if I could be any food, I'd probably be pasta. I'd be this pasta one hundred percent," she rambles. "Babe, if I were pasta would you eat me?"

Dani hides her laughter at Ri's antics in the crook of her elbow.

"I would a hunnid percent eat you if you were pasta, Ri. You'd be so delicious as pasta."

"Right? I'd be the best pasta ever," she giggles behind her hand. High Ri is the best Ri.

She goes to fix a second plate, but I stop her. "You sure you wanna eat more of the THC food, Ri? You don't wanna take a break and eat regular food for a minute?"

"I'm so hungry, sis. I'm soooo hungry."

"I know, so you can eat the regular food if you want, but you're sitting real nice with your high right now. I don't think you should push it."

She starts rapping the words to "Push It" by Salt N Pepa, making me wonder if she somehow snuck some alcohol that I didn't see before. I guess we can chalk it up to the fact that she never gets high and let her have her moment.

"I think there's..." she cuts herself off, turning to look at whatever imaginary thing just whizzed by her, and when she turns back to me, she must forget she was speaking because she doesn't say a word.

"Okay, go eat, Ri."

She literally perks up at the use of the word 'eat' and then piles her plate high with more infused food.

I shake my head, thanking God that Arnold is the one who has to deal with her tonight. I'll take the fun Ri, not the past her limits Ri, nor the hungover Ri that's bound to visit us tomorrow.

Evie leaves dinner without so much as a goodbye, but texts me that she was so sleepy and her bed was calling her so at least I know she's safe.

With everyone impaired, no one pays attention to Rome and me, so we walk back to my room hand in hand.

"How you holding up?" I ask once he closes my door.

"I should be asking you that, your eyes are barely open."

I chuckle, walking toward him until we're face to face. "I'm feeling really good."

"Good."

"Mhm, I could feel even better, though."

"How so?"

"A little birdie told me that you're the reason I got to swim with sea turtles today. Is that the case?"

He shrugs nonchalantly.

"Don't do that."

"Do what?"

"Minimize the effect you have on my happiness. That made my day today."

"Whatever you need and want, whenever you need and want it. I'm not gonna repeat myself again, J."

His tone hits me right in my core, sending my need for him into overdrive. If tonight is the last night we have, I want to make the most of it.

"Well, what I want right now is to properly thank you for making today happen."

He pulls me against his body, gripping my ass with both hands. "What'd you have in mind?"

"You like to play with the senses, so I thought I'd give that a try myself."

"And what are you gonna do?"

"Don't ask questions. Now, I'm gonna put my headphones on you so that I can get what I need without you hearing. And I want you to close your eyes."

"What are you up to?"

"Oh, so I can repeat myself, but you can't? I said no questions."

"But…"

"Aht aht aht," I scold. "My thank you, my rules."

"Yes ma'am. I hear you, no questions."

"Thank you. I'll tap your arm when you can open your eyes so go ahead and close them." He closes his eyes and adjusts my earbuds so they're comfortable for him.

I rush to grab ice from my freezer and puts them into a cup, running them under cold water in the sink.

I take a minute to observe him, looking edible in his tan pants and blue polo, the imprint of his abs strong against his shirt. I circle him, careful to step lightly so he doesn't know where I am and then I stand in front of him, so close our breaths mingle. I can still smell the pecan pie Highly Catered served for dessert on his tongue.

I reach for his pants, taking my time to unbutton them and pull them down painstakingly slowly. Acting on instinct, he steps out of the pants, kicking them aside, narrowly missing the cup of ice I have on the floor beside me.

Popping an ice cube into my mouth, I hide the cup behind me, clamp my mouth shut, and tap his arm. He opens his eyes suspiciously, but any unasked questions fall to the wayside when I sink to my knees before him. I motion for him to take the earbuds out and without any further pomp and circumstance, I take him in my mouth.

The wet heat of my mouth mingled with the chill of the ice sends a shock to his system and he jumps in my hold.

"Ah fuck," he groans. I use my lips to suction the ice to the base of his dick and trail it up and down. His hands fly to the back of my head, his fingers stinging my scalp with a bite of pain. I welcome it, knowing it's his lifeline because I'm pushing him to the brink of insanity. The ice starts to melt rapidly in my mouth so I let it pool there, taking him down my throat as far as I can.

I gag around him, some of the water dripping down my chin and when I meet his eyes his knees buckle for a second.

"You're a demon. Oh shit," he groans, his head falling backward when his dick touches my tonsils.

When the rest of the ice melts, I swirl my tongue around his base before slowly pulling him from my mouth.

"You can take it right, Rome?"

His teeth sink into his bottom lip as he soothes my scalp with the pads of his fingers.

I grab another ice cube from my cup, rubbing it along my hand.

"Damn, J."

"Make me proud, Rome," I tease as I grab the base of his dick with the ice still in my hand, massaging what doesn't fit in my mouth.

He stomps his foot in approval, no longer bothering with words but his body tells me everything I need to know.

I alternate between sucking his balls into my mouth and massaging them with the ice, never letting Rome get comfortable with the sensation.

"J, I'm gonna come," his warning comes through clenched teeth.

I take him to the base of my throat, not wanting to waste a single drop, and when his release coats my tongue I show him the evidence of what I did to him before I swallow it down.

He huffs out a harsh breath, wiping a bead of sweat from his brow. "Now, that's a thank you I would accept from you any day."

He bends down to scoop me up, and so begins the cycle of properly thanking each other.

"Shit, what time is it?" I ask, checking my phone to see it's three a.m. We fell asleep tangled up in each other but the reminder of our impending doom jolts me awake.

"You got somewhere to be?"

"No, but I meant to give you your gift."

He wiggles his eyebrows at the mention of a gift. "You gotta give me ten more minutes for another gift or thank you, you took me out that last round."

"Shut your ass up." I shimmy from under his hold to grab the clay turtles from my bag. I climb back under the covers and present them to him with a bright smile.

"Oh wow, that's so cool. It's me and you," he says, awestruck.

"That's what I thought."

He moves a rogue braid that fell across my eyelid. "And they're together."

"They could be mating. Then it really would be us," I laugh.

"Thank you, J. I appreciate this."

"You're welcome. I wanted to get you something to tell you how much the past week meant to me. I thought this would be a great goodbye gift."

He sits up in alarm, the bedsheet falling off his naked torso. "Goodbye gift?"

"Yeah. Today is officially wedding week."

He laughs though his face remains unsmiling. "Right."

"Rome. We said one week."

"No, you said that."

"You agreed!"

"Because it was that or nothing! I'm man enough to admit I made a mistake. I shouldn't have agreed to one week when I really wanted two."

"It's just not possible."

He huffs. "Of course, it is. You're just too scared to go for it."

The truth of that draws the line in the sand between us. I'm too scared and he's not scared enough so there's nowhere else for us to go.

He waits for me to say something, anything, but I don't have anything to give. Nothing I say in this moment would change where we are. If we stand any chance of not damaging all the wonderful memories we made together this week, the best thing I can do is stay silent.

Realizing I'm not going to be the one to break the silence, he gets up from the bed and starts putting his clothes on.

"You don't have to leave," I say, panic seizing my bones.

"Yeah, I do. We're back to being friends, right? I wouldn't be in your room at three in the morning as just your friend so it's best I go. I'll see you tomorrow." He gives me one final forehead kiss and stops in the doorway on his way out. "Thank you for the turtles."

PART TWO

THE STORM

CHAPTER EIGHT

Rome

"**W**HERE THE FUCK IS MY RING?!"

My eyes creep open at the sound of thunderous yelling outside of my room.

Sleep was just starting to come to me after evading me the entire morning after I left Janelle's room, and now this shit.

Pulling on some sweats I walk over to the door and peer out to see Amerie pacing back and forth, her hands waving animatedly.

"Babe, calm down. We're gonna find it."

"Calm down!? The fuck? My ring is missing and you telling me to calm down? You're not upset it's gone!?"

"It's not gone. It's around here somewhere."

"It better be and everybody needs to help look for it." She lifts her hand up to knock on my door, but I pull it open before she gets a chance.

"Morning."

Arnold scratches the back of his neck and Amerie offers a tight smile. "Morning, Rome. My ring is missing so I'm asking for all hands on deck to find it."

"What the hell is going on?" We turn toward Janelle who is rounding the corner with Dani beside her.

Janelle looks beautiful as always, but looking closely at her eyes, I see how tired they look. They're red around the rim, slightly puffy underneath. Her shoulders seem heavy with weight and like the fool I am my first and only thought is how to take it from her.

"We heard you yelling from our rooms. What is happening?" Dani asks.

"My fucking ring is missing!" Amerie exclaims, her hands flying to her hips. I'm amazed at her sheer audacity to look like she's tired of telling everyone about her ring, as if she's not asking for our help to find it.

"How is that possible?"

"You think I know?!"

"Well, wasn't it on your finger last?" Janelle asks.

Amerie sneers at Janelle. A deep crease forms in the middle of her forehead as her eyes sink to impossibly low slits. "I must have taken it off after y'all got me high as a kite and now it's gone."

"I think I remember Janelle telling you not to eat that second portion," I chime in. Amerie grimaces at my words but doesn't address me. Interesting.

A smirk graces Janelle's face but it's gone as soon as it appears.

She and Dani exchange a look and turn to Amerie like she's a wounded animal they're trying to coax into their arms.

"Okay, it's fine. We'll help you find it. You don't have any memory of taking it off?"

Steam practically shoots through her nostrils before she exhales through her mouth and speaks. "I don't. I just realized it wasn't on my finger when I woke up this morning. I just need…" her voice cracks as she pinches the bridge of her nose and heaves out a sob.

Arnold, Janelle, and Dani all freeze at the sight of Amerie's tears but they don't move me.

She's the one who lost her ring, but she came to us demanding we help her find it, and when she was called out for being rude she resorted to tears instead of just correcting the behavior. It doesn't sit right with me. I haven't taken the time I probably should have as Arnold's friend getting to know Amerie, but I'm unimpressed with what I've seen during this trip and what I saw during the engagement party.

Arnold wraps Amerie up in his arms, kissing the top of her head. "Babe, why don't you go lay down. We'll look for it."

Oh, we will?

"No, I can't sleep 'til I find it. I just need everyone to help me."

"Okay, so how bout you go get Eve, Christian, and Micah to go with you? I'll stay with this group, and we'll divide and conquer."

The color drains from Amerie's face as she looks back and forth between Arnold and Janelle. Arnold is standing in front of Amerie so Janelle can't see the scathing look on her sister's face, but I can. My hackles rise with the clear discomfort she feels with leaving the two of them together. Who is she implying can't be trusted? Her man or her sister?

Neither answer is acceptable.

Arnold offers her a reassuring smile and squeezes her hand. She blinks and literally shakes it off, offering him a warm smile. "Yeah. Okay that works. I'll go find everyone else." She looks past Arnold to Janelle and Dani. "Why didn't Evie come with y'all anyway?"

"Now you know her ass could sleep through a hurricane," Dani laughs.

Amerie doesn't crack so much as a smile at Dani's comment. "Yeah, you're right. Okay, good luck looking guys. I'll call to check in."

Amerie walks toward Janelle toward where Eve and the guys' rooms are, when Janelle snakes her hand out to grab Amerie's wrist. "It's gonna be okay, sis."

She looks down at where their arms connect briefly then detangles herself from Janelle's grasp. "I'll believe that when we find it."

With that, she walks off leaving Janelle staring at the back of her head and Dani hanging her head.

"Follow me, I know where to start," Arnold waves us on.

He leads us to the patio where the rehearsal dinner was held and spins around to face us, rolling his shoulders back and holding his head up high. "Okay, after dinner when y'all left we stayed behind and danced around so it could've fallen off here." He puts a British spin on his voice, pulling a laugh out of both Janelle and me.

"Oh, shit. Not Sherlock Black on the scene," I say, cackling.

Janelle's laugh becomes even louder. "Oh my God, Sherlock Black is wild. I used to call him Luther." Arnold grins at her former nickname for him.

"That's a good one. I would never compliment him by comparing him to Idris, though."

"I'm so confused. Someone fill me in," Dani interrupts.

"Arnold loses stuff all the time." The man can make millions of dollars for athletes in his sleep but can't keep track of his keys, phone, or wallet.

Janelle chimes in to finish the explanation. "And when he does, he has this whole bit where he becomes a British detective while he retraces his steps to find whatever he lost."

"Hence Sherlock Black," I finish.

Dani tilts her head at Arnold and snickers. "Men are so dumb."

"Facts. Okay, so around here?" Janelle waves her hand around the patio area and Arnold nods.

"Yep. Specifically, right here," he stands in a spot two feet away from the now empty table. "So, if it fell off her finger it probably would've rolled around this side."

Dani blinks rapidly, her mouth slightly ajar. "Are you...gonna do that accent the entire time?"

Janelle laughs and throws her arm around Dani's shoulder. "I learned it's best to just let him go through the motions." She leads her away from Arnold and I, toward the surrounding palm trees.

"What say you, Watson? Shall we look over yonder whilst the womenfolk scour the far side?"

Grinning at the first sight of my real friend, I stand taller and adjust my imaginary tie. "I say that's a splendid idea, ol chap."

We comb through every inch of the patio, coming up empty handed. Arnold starts grumbling to himself, trying to remember where he and Amerie went after dinner and the next moment, he takes off.

"Oop, he's on the move. Let's go, people," Janelle directs.

We follow Arnold to the pool area, and he stalks around it with one hand behind his back and the other grazing his beard.

"Bet money he says 'according to my calculations' in the next five minutes," Janelle whispers to me. Her braids, hanging loose and framing her face, lightly strokes my arm. She uses my wrist to steady herself so I use my other hand to pull her closer to me. The heat pouring off her at my touch threatens to engulf us both in the flames.

"I think I'd be a fool to take that bet."

"True, you would. So, over or under on the five minutes?"

I look over to Arnold, still pacing the pool and wait for the tell-tale sign of him checking his watch. When he does, I turn to Janelle with a gleeful grin. "Under. I give it two minutes, max."

Dani taps her foot and claps her hands, gaining all our attention. "Is this still part of the process? Are we waiting for the ring to call to us or something?"

Arnold motions for us to come closer, so we form a huddle around him. "After we left the patio, she really wanted to sit and watch the water but insisted the pool in our room didn't give off the right vibe, so we came here. She sat in every single chair testing their quote unquote comfort levels then she stared into space for a while before she stripped off all her clothes and jumped in. Things get a little x rated from there so Ima shut up but yeah."

"It's this raggedy British accent for me. Okay, so she sat in every single chair on both sides of the pool?" Dani asks.

"No, just this side. And this," he points to a chair right in the center. "Is the one she chose so according to my calculations; it should have ended up right here."

Janelle looks at me, grabbing my arm with an iron tight grip and we both fall into a fit of laughter. She bends over with a cough, bumping the chair in question with her hip and moving it closer to the edge of the pool. "Shit, I can't breathe."

My laughter grows louder as I bring my hand to her back to help her stand back up. "What I tell you? Two minutes on the dot."

She wipes a few tears away from her eyes and giggles again. "You know, Arnold, I always wanted to ask you. What exactly goes into those calculations of yours? What's the science behind it?"

"Bout to start calling you TI-83."

Janelle slaps my arm as another fit of laughter takes over her. "Yo on his Velma shit, talkin bout some 'according to my calculations.'"

"Ol' Mystery Machine lookin ass."

At this point, Dani joins in on the laughter while Arnold does his best to look irritated with us. He presses his lips into a wobbly hard line.

"You wanna tell us the wind projections from last night too?" Janelle asks, licking her finger and holding it up to the nonexistent wind.

Dani lets out a snort which only makes Janelle and I laugh harder.

"Ayo, fuck y'all. My methods always work."

"That's not true. Remember when you lost your coffee mug while we were out shopping and you never found it?" Janelle asks.

He shakes his head and points his finger at her. "I stand by it, someone at Tumi stole my damn mug."

"And I kept telling you, nobody wanted that busted ass mug."

"It was a nice mug!"

"Was it though? It was literally chipped on the side."

"It gave it character."

Janelle's eyebrows spike up to her hairline as she mouths 'character' and Arnold chuckles. This is the first time I've witnessed them acknowledge that they meant something to each other once upon a time. Janelle looks unphased by it, but Arnold visibly relaxes with the interaction, like it's taken a huge weight off his shoulders to not have to pretend that Janelle is nothing more than his fiancé's sister.

"Whatever, it works ninety-nine percent of the time. I bet we gonna find it right here."

"I'll take that bet." I would bet my last dollar on the ring not being here. Truth be told, I wouldn't be surprised if Amerie took that ring off on purpose just to give Janelle something else to do.

"Bet. How much we talkin…"

His words are cut off by the sound of Amerie hollering. She storms around the corner with Christian, Micah, and Eve lagging behind her.

"Hey babe, how's the search going?"

She squints at him, power walking over to him. Her breathing is labored and her steps are unsure. "We found it," she says unceremoniously.

Arnold's face lights up and he plants his hands on her shoulders. "That's great! Where was it?"

"Y'all's room," Eve chips in.

The news confirms what I'd been thinking all morning. I should've had Arnold bet me at least a million.

"Our room? You checked our room this morning. How'd you miss it?"

"Micah found it. It was underneath the bed between the post and the wall," Christian adds.

The group goes silent. I'm quite sure everyone is starting to mirror my thoughts. *Is she really sitting here telling us that she didn't think to look under her bed? And if she did, she somehow missed the big ass diamond Arnold laced her finger with sitting against the wall?*

Arnold clears his throat. "Well, that's great. I told you it was around here somewhere."

"Oh, is that why you seemed so unconcerned?"

"What?"

"It just seemed like you were having a lot of fun not looking for my ring."

Eve guffaws and Janelle moves closer to her, effectively removing herself from Amerie's line of sight.

"We were looking for it. Ask Rome and Janelle. I was using my detective skills to retrace our steps, that's why we're here."

Micah and Christian laugh, I'm sure at the image of Sherlock Black they know so well, but Amerie's face only constricts more.

"I don't wanna ask Janelle anything about you."

Record scratch.

I've had enough of this bullshit. Amerie has tested the limits of my kindness and I'm learning that where Janelle is concerned, they don't extend far in the first place.

"Amerie?" She turns at the sound of my voice. "I think the words you're looking for are thank you."

"Excuse me?"

"I think what you wanna be doing right now is thanking everyone for taking time out of their morning to help you look for something you lost. Whatever this is you're doing? We can skip it."

"Rome, no offense..."

I cut her off. "None taken. I'm sure you didn't mean to come off rude as fuck to your fiancé, your sister, and your friends. It's okay, shit happens. It's been a stressful morning, so we can just accept your thank you and move on. Right, y'all?"

Micah and Dani stay absolutely still and quiet. Christian laughs while nodding. Eve applauds profusely while Janelle stares at me, stunned. Arnold gauges Amerie's reaction, running his hand down her arm comfortingly.

"Uh, right. Yeah. Thanks everyone. I appreciate your help." Her jaw clenches and her fists tighten. It physically pains her to say this. "Arnold, we should get going. We need to pick up my parents soon and I wanted to stop to get Mommy some flowers on the way."

Janelle perks up, stepping back into Amerie's field of view. "Ooh, what time should I meet y'all in the lobby?"

Amerie cranks her head to Janelle quickly, turns to Arnold, and then back at Janelle. "What do you mean?"

"I mean what time are we leaving for the airport?"

"We?" Amerie asks.

"You hard of hearing now? Yes, we. When I talked to Dad, he said he expected me to be at the airport with you to greet him."

Amerie rolls her eyes and I see her starting to pick her thumb by her side. She rolls her shoulders back and clears her throat. "It's just that Arnold and I were gonna take them around for a bit before we get settled. Probably go to lunch."

Janelle's eye twitches and I wish I were closer so I could help calm her nerves. What is it about this woman that makes me want to walk through fire just so she doesn't burn? "So, I can't come with y'all?"

"You'd wanna be the fifth wheel?"

"With my parents and my sister? I wouldn't think I'd feel like a fifth wheel in that situation."

I look at Arnold, waiting for him to get involved but he's back to being the guy that just sits around, letting this shit happen.

"Ri, what the fuck? Why can't she just come?" Eve asks, stomping her foot.

"It's all good, Evie," Janelle assures her with her palm up.

"No, it's not. Because you starting to piss me off, Ri."

"What the hell did I do?"

"You've been acting shady with Nelly all week."

Amerie's nostrils flare and she cranes her neck toward Janelle. "Is that how you feel?"

A war rages in Janelle's eyes. Yes, surrounded by our friends on an empty stomach with the humidity bearing down on us probably isn't the best place for her and Amerie to have it out, but this is a moment that probably won't come around again. She looks at me briefly and I will her to acknowledge her true feelings, but the deep exhale she lets out lets me know she's not about to do that.

"I don't wanna fight, Ri. I just want you to have the best wedding."

Beside me, I hear Dani let out a somber sigh. Everyone is growing tired of Amerie's bullshit, but everyone knows it has to be Janelle who puts her in her place.

"See, she disagrees."

"Ri, stop," Dani barks.

"That's not what the fuck she said, Ri," Eve's words come out as a harsh growl. If Janelle isn't willing to lean on me this week, I'm glad she has Eve and Dani in her corner.

"Okay, that's enough," Arnold, now deciding to use his vocal cords, interrupts.

I step in before he can put his foot further down his throat. Holding up my hand to stop all conversation, I address Janelle directly. "J, I'm pretty sure my brother is on the same flight as your parents, and I have to pick him up so you can ride with me that way you don't have to be where you aren't wanted."

Arnold hangs his head as Amerie scoffs. "That's not…" The look I send Amerie's way cuts off any rebuttal that was threatening to jump off her tongue. "Well, it looks like Rome solved the problem, so there we go."

Christian lets out a whistle as he and Micah back away slowly.

"I like you." Eve pats me on the back, grabbing Dani and pulling her away from the group. Arnold gives Amerie a tentative kiss and then guides her out as well, leaving me alone with Janelle.

"You didn't have to do that but I'm glad you did. Thank you."

I don't even respond. I just tip my head to her and make my way to the car.

After driving almost two hours to the airport in comfortable silence and then sitting for thirty minutes with Arnold and Amerie in uncomfortable silence, a man that could very well be Janelle's twin exits the terminal. Janelle is up and running toward him before I can even point him out.

He scoops her up in a bear hug and plants a kiss on her cheek. A shorter woman with a short pixie cut, who I assume is her mother, stands beside them, watching with a smile. Amerie grabs Arnold's hand and drags him over to join the welcome wagon.

I see my brother exit the terminal, flagged by an overenthusiastic white man. The look in Jalen's eyes screams 'save me' so I jog over to greet him.

We pull each other into a bro hug and when Jalen starts talking to me without acknowledging the man, he gets the hint and leaves.

"Excited fan?"

"He talked the whole damn flight. Gave me a dissertation on why the sport needs me back and why I should specifically look to play for LA; Apparently, Tyson Richards and I would make a dynamic duo."

Jalen is a NBA legend. He played for the Washington Bullets, bringing home four championship rings, four MVP awards, and three Olympic gold medals. Three years ago, at the age of thirty-five he shocked the world by announcing that he was retiring from the game. While he made it clear that his decision was final, only our family knew the reason behind his retirement was issues with his ex-wife causing him to need to dedicate all his time to being a dad, so fans have continued to hold out hope that he'll one day return.

"Tyson is a beast though," I shrug.

He glowers at me. "And he don't need my old ass to win a championship." Arnold walks over and daps Jalen up. The two of them catch up for a moment before the Cross family reaches us.

"Mom, Dad, you remember Rome, right? And this, I assume, is his brother Jalen," Janelle smiles. She greets Jalen and his normally non-hugging ass immediately wraps her up in a hug like he's known her for years.

"Yes, of course. I forgot there's two of you though. Good lord, your poor mama," Mrs. Cross shakes her head. When I met her at the engagement party, she was floored by mine and Micah's height.

When I told her my mom is five-foot-eleven and my dad is six-foot-ten she sent a prayer out for my mom, saying she was brave to be willing to push not one but two big headed giant children into this world.

"You'll have to excuse her. Everyone is tall to her," Mr. Cross teases. Mrs. Cross stands at about five-foot-three so I'm sure there's some merit to that.

I cover her hand with mine. "It's nice to see you again, Mrs. Cross."

She waves me off with a charming smile. "Oh, please. Deb or Debbie is just fine, baby." She exchanges pleasantries with Jalen and then we head toward baggage claim.

I trail behind the group, watching the interactions between Janelle and her parents. Her mom constantly frets over her, asking how she's holding up and wanting details on how the trip's been so far. She doesn't outright ask if things are awkward with her and Arnold but her continuous looks over her shoulder at Arnold makes it obvious. Her dad seems to notice the hunch in Janelle's shoulders and pulls her under his arm, testing a bunch of new dad jokes on her which gets her laughing.

"I don't know about y'all but I'm starving, and I know y'all wouldn't wanna see an old man wither away so let's get a move on."

"Charles, you act like you didn't eat a full meal right before we got on the plane and about four bags of pretzels on the plane."

"I don't know nothing bout that. What I know is I need some food and I need it now." He pats his stomach for dramatic effect.

"Well, that's perfect. Arnold and I wanted to take you to lunch before heading to the hotel, anyway."

Charles stops in his tracks. "Just you and Arnold? You're not coming, Nugget?" He asks Janelle.

Amerie practically jumps in her dad's arms, blocking his view of Janelle. "Well, Daddy, it's just that Arnold and I wanted to treat you and Mommy to a nice lunch before the wedding festivities kick off."

"Now, Bug, you can still do that with your sister in tow. How you gonna invite us to lunch and not invite your sister? And Rome and Jalen. Y'all must be hungry, too." The respect I have for Charles Cross instantly goes up a few notches.

"Daddy, don't worry about it. I've got stuff to do anyway so I can't come." It kills me to watch her bow down to Amerie's every whim. If anyone else had pulled half the shit Amerie has, Janelle would've destroyed them, so this power Amerie seems to hold over her is unnerving.

"Charles, don't make a big deal out of it. Janelle doesn't need this on her plate," Deb admonishes.

"For fuck's sake," Janelle mumbles under her breath.

We hurriedly say goodbye and get the hell out of there. When we get to the car Janelle reaches for the backseat handle.

"Janelle, what the hell are you doing?"

"Getting in the car," she quips, confusion framing her features.

"I see that. Why are you getting in the back?"

She rolls her eyes. "Because your brother is here now so there's no reason for me to be up front."

I place my hand on top of the one she has resting on the door handle and lower my voice so only she can hear me. "Unless I'm laying you down and driving you to the brink of insanity with my dick you should never see the backseat of my car. Get your ass to the front."

She shivers under my touch, crossing one ankle in front of the other. "Why are you like this?"

"Ask Rochelle Martin."

She rolls her eyes. "Well, your mama ain't here so..." she waves her free hand as if that will make me let her go.

I press my body closer into hers. She gasps when she feels my length against her side. "You want me to call her? Put your pretty ass on FaceTime so she can tell you the kind of man she raised?"

"You are not bout to call your mama on me."

"You keep thinking I'm not bout that action, J. I've proved you wrong before and I'ma keep doing so."

She licks her bottom lip but straightens when I blatantly let my eyes follow the action. "Damn. Yep, you win this round."

"Let's not talk about rounds, J. One week was plenty, ain't that what you said?"

"Aaaand with that." She pushes against my chest and I let her go, following her to the passenger side so I can open her door for her.

I hear Jalen's low rumble of laughter as he lets himself into the backseat.

An hour into our drive back, Janelle and Jalen have been going back and forth with questions to get to know each other better. I can't lie and say it doesn't make my heart happy to see my brother and my...and Janelle getting along so well.

"So, is Kam ready for a week without you?"

"He's with our parents so he's not even gonna notice I'm gone. Our mom will probably buy him ten video games and our dad will probably let him stay up all hours of the night to watch scary movies."

"And Mom's gonna yell at him to send Kam to bed but she's always the first one to fall asleep; she ain't gonna do shit about it," I add in.

"Exactly that."

"He's got the grandparents working against each other; he's a genius. He's into scary movies?"

"He loves 'em. He probably shouldn't be watching them since he's only eleven, but my dad got him started early."

"See, now that we can talk about. I leave the horror games to Evie but horror movies? Sign me up."

"Oh yeah? What's your favorite?"

"*Nightmare on Elm Street* first. *Halloween* sits at a close second."

"Kam would approve. Michael Myers is his guy."

"I knew I liked him."

We get back to the hotel and Janelle tells us she's going to go rest while Amerie is gone but promises to see us at the tequila tasting later tonight.

"So that's my future sister-in-law, huh? I like her," Jalen spews the moment she's out of sight.

"The fuck are you talking about?"

"Shorty got you wide open, my guy. You can't deny that."

He doesn't even know about the past week I've spent with her, but he has me pegged. It's way too early to claim her as my wife, but I know without a shadow of a doubt that I want more with Janelle, and I'm willing to do what it takes to make her see that, too.

Later that night, Arnold's parents and a few other guests have arrived and Amerie and Arnold have invited everyone to a tequila tasting as a welcome.

They booked a bus to take us to and from the restaurant where the tasting is being held so that everyone can let loose.

It takes everything in me not to pull Janelle into my arms when she meets us in the lobby dressed in a gold satin ruched dress that hugs her curves and strappy heels that wrap around her calves. I'd rather be tasting her tonight than any brand of tequila. My mind keeps floating, imagining what it would be like to be with her out loud. To be able to touch her unabashedly because everyone knows we belong to each other. I'm going through withdrawals. Desperate to feel her body wrapped around me, the sound of her pleasure playing on a loop in my ear.

When we get to the restaurant, we're escorted to a large private room decorated in all whites, greens, and golds. A table in the back is adorned with a feast consisting of all different kinds of tacos, ceviche, nachos, and grilled vegetables. A woman with tan skin and dark hair stands behind a table surrounded by flight paddles, grinning wide.

"Welcome, everyone. Come on in. I'm Maria and I'll be your tequila master tonight. Please grab a bite and enjoy. We'll get started shortly."

Once everyone has had a few minutes to eat and chat, she jumps right into the tasting. Introducing one tequila or mezcal after another and describing the flavors, aromas, and physical traits of each one. She walks us through the proper way to observe and study tequila before tasting it, giving nuance to the entire experience.

Dani is enthralled by Maria's presentation skills, most likely plotting how she can steal her away to work for her at Promesa. Janelle seems to thoroughly enjoy the tasting experience, taking the time to note the flavors she's able to pick up on and ask questions about what she missed before indulging. Everything she does, she does with fervor. She dives into it completely and dedicates her all to it. If only I could get her to do that with us.

After the official tasting is over, everyone is left to enjoy the drinks and food for a while as the bus won't be back to get us for another hour.

Janelle and I have avoided each other tonight, keeping to our respective bubbles but when we bump into each other in the center of the room, I happily burst it.

"Did you learn anything new tonight?" she asks.

"I've learned a lot about a lot of things."

She chuckles. "What does that even mean?"

"Nothing. Just that I'm watching and learning."

She looks me up and down, assessing em carefully. "Of that I have no doubt, Rome."

"Nelly, oh my gosh!" A drunken Amerie stumbles over to where Janelle and I stand, a young looking Black man standing behind her.

"Are you okay, Ri?"

"Me? I'm great." She lowers her voice to a mock whisper. "I have someone I want you to meet." She flops her hands in the air behind her, inspiring the mystery guy to step out from behind her.

"Nelly, this is Troy. Troy, this is my sister, Nelly. Or Janelle. Troy is Arnold's protege. He's gonna be a great agent one day."

She winks at Janelle, who's standing there looking like a deer in headlights. "Yeah, it's nice to meet you, Troy."

"Likewise," he takes her hand in his and kisses it. I'm not sure if the gagging sound I hear is from her or me.

"Troy doesn't have a date for the ceremony."

"Okay…" Janelle drags out the word.

"And neither do you."

"Well, I'm in the ceremony so I'm not sure why I need a date."

"For after, silly." Her words begin to slur a little harder.

"No one in the wedding party has dates. Not uncommon for a destination wedding, sis."

She puts her fingers over her mouth, signaling Janelle to lower her voice. "I know. I know. I know. But I just thought you two might hit it off. Maybe you should go somewhere private and talk," she suggests. She gestures toward the exit but the movement throws her off balance, so I reach my hand up to steady her.

"I don't think that's necessary," Janelle starts.

"Oh my gosh, great idea, Nelly. Okay, I'm gonna go mingle since it is my wedding and all. Have fun you two!" She sings as she scurries away, ignoring all the protests flying out of Janelle's mouth.

This guy looks no older than twenty-three and that's being generous. It's cute that Amerie thinks he'd be a good date for Janelle at the wedding, but it's not happening. Simple as that.

"I'm so sorry about that. She means well," Janelle apologizes to Troy. I notice him lick his lips as he takes Janelle in.

"Hey, I mean, she might be onto something. I'm not opposed to having a date for the wedding." He looks at me as if just remembering I'm standing here. "Do you want to grab another drink?"

Janelle looks to me, eyes wide. Pain flashes across her face and she slides her hands down her sides. "Uh, sure. Let's just step over here." She lays her hand on the middle of his back and guides him to an empty cocktail table.

When she turns back to me, she mouths the words 'I'm sorry', driving the knife in a little deeper.

CHAPTER NINE

Janelle

I'M PAST READY FOR THIS DAMN WEDDING TO BE OVER.

Ri thinking she could force a date on me was the last straw for me. I had to remind myself to be the lady my daddy raised me to be, so I didn't cuss her drunk dumb ass out in front of her guests.

I pulled Troy aside last night so I could tell him I wasn't interested and apologize for Ri wasting his time. On the surface there's nothing wrong with Troy. He's handsome, he's tall, and he has a nice body with honey brown skin. He's too young for my taste, only being twenty-four, but if I had met him before the trip, sans the ambush from Ri, I may have taken his number. Unfortunately for Troy, he has one major thing working against him: he's not Rome.

That man has ruined me for the rest of this vacation. If it's not going to be him beating up my walls, then I guess I'm going out sad because my kitty is not purring for anyone else. I knew I should've just packed one of my toys. Toys are way less complicated. They don't talk back. They don't leave you wondering what could've been. They don't make you question all your decisions. You get all the pleasure with none of the headache.

The last thing I want to be doing today is spending time with Ri and others doing an ATV tour, yet here we are. Oh, well. Maybe the bumps along the trail will give me the friction I'm sorely missing.

I look around to see what group I'm stuck with today. With fifty guests, there's no way we can do every activity together. Ri arranged smaller group activities so that everyone could participate in the things she planned and could get a chance to see each other prior to the ceremony. Right now, ten of us are about to go on this ATV jungle and cenote tour while other groups are ziplining, shopping, or living it up at a day party.

I roll my eyes when I see Troy in the group, no chance that was a coincidence. The rest of the crew seems to be the usual suspects—Evie, Rome, Ri, Arnold, Dani, Micah, Jalen, and…shit.

"Jesus be a fence," I hiss.

Evie, who had wandered in front of me, whips around when she hears me. "Uh oh. I know shit ain't right when you start throwing out the church phrases. What's wrong?"

I step closer to her, keeping my eye on the subject at hand. I don't want him to sneak up on me. "You see the dumbass standing next to Arnold?"

She sneaks a peek in that direction and looks back at me with a curious expression. "The guy with the swole shoulders who looks like he's never seen a leg day in his life? Yeah, who is he?"

"That's Arnold's cousin, Cortez. I knew he was invited to the wedding, but I didn't realize he RSVP'd. I met him once and decided that was one time too many. I'm not prepared to deal with his ass today." He lives in Chicago, so I never had to worry about running into him after that awful first encounter, but he left a bad taste in my mouth.

"Well, is he gonna be a problem? Because you don't need Jesus to be the fence. I'm the fence and I wish a motherfucker would try to get through me." She puffs out her chest, trying to make her five-foot-seven, one-hundred-and-fifty-pound frame seem intimidating. That's how she gets you, though. She looks so sweet and innocent, but she will cut the heads off her enemies without breaking a sweat.

"I'm good, Evie. I swear. You know I know how to deal with fools, I just would rather not. Be prepared for him to try to talk to you though. He's about to treat this wedding like his personal playground."

"Please. I don't waste time on men whose knees would buckle if he tried to pick me up. Hard pass."

I snort out a laugh. A tour guide comes to Ri to introduce himself as Jaime and to ask her how many ATVs will be needed as they offer both single and double riders.

"Oh, I'm gonna ride with Arnold so that's one double." Her head swivels around our group and when her eyes land on me, they light up. "Nelly, how about you? You want to ride with a partner?" She inclines her head toward Troy in the most obvious manner, making me ball my fist up by my side.

Troy looks at me sympathetically but stays silent. I could just ride with him to get Ri off my back but I'm beyond tired of making concessions for her. The well of my patience has run dry. Something has to give and for once it's not going to be me.

I try to look over at Rome but Cortez steps in my way. "Oh shit. Janelle, Janelle, Janelle. I didn't recognize you at first. It's been a while." *Not long enough.* "You look good as fuck, girl."

"Mhm, thank you."

"You're more than welcome to ride on the back of my ATV. I'll give you the ride of your life." He sways on his feet, laughing at his own joke, but his movement allows me to see Rome narrow his eyes at him. I'm surprised the back of Cortez's head isn't melting with the heat Rome is sending his way. Frankly, everyone looks unimpressed with him, but it seems to go completely over his big ass head.

Not even bothering to respond to him, I turn my focus to Jaime. "I'll drive by myself, thanks." I hear Ri suck her teeth, but she recovers quickly, giving Troy an apologetic smile and shaking off her disappointment in me. Cortez winks at me as he moves closer to Dani.

When my eyes find Rome again, he allows me to see the pride on his face for a split second before he turns away.

Rome, Micah, Dani, and Troy all opt to ride alone as well, but in a surprise turn of events Evie and Jalen opt to ride together. We're all given our gear and Jalen helps her secure her helmet.

We're given a brief safety demo before we take off. The jungle trail is beautiful. Surrounded by nothing but greenery for as far as we can see it feels like we've been transported to our own personal paradise. Even with the sand raining down on me from the ATV in front of me, I still feel at peace. The bullshit of this trip rolls off my back in waves.

We make a stop along the way so that Jalen can switch spots with Evie and so Arnold can do the same with Ri. Cortez tries to ride his ATV over to me, but Rome cuts him off, planting his ATV between us and looking straight ahead as if he didn't notice him. I purse my lips together to hold in my laugh, following Rome's lead by looking straight ahead.

"Okay, we're going to leave our vehicles right here on this side. There's a bathroom where you can wash up or change if you aren't already wearing your swimsuit up ahead. Those of you who are already changed, head this way to get your new helmets, flashlights, and water shoes," Jaime announces once we reach the cave entrance.

Dani, Evie, and I head for the bathrooms to change but a hand grips my arm, pulling me back. Ri forces her arm through mine, trying to make it look like two sisters walking lovingly together rather than a mother scolding her disobedient child. "Umm, what do you need, Ri?"

"You're completely ignoring Troy. What is that about?"

I stop in my tracks and pull my arm free from hers. "That is about the fact that I'm not interested in Troy."

"Ugh, why not? He's perfect for you."

"How so?"

"What?" She stutters.

"What makes him so perfect for me, Ri?"

"Well, he's successful. He's cute. He's nice. He's a good guy! You're not even giving him a chance."

"And won't. I mean, that is the bare minimum, Ri. By that description he'd be perfect for literally anyone here, and there are plenty of single women at this wedding to choose from. So, get somebody else to do it and stop wasting my time."

"Nelly, I just want…"

"Let it go, Ri. Before you get your feelings hurt." I hurry to catch up with Dani and Evie, not sparing her another glance.

After everyone regathers, we enter the gorgeous Cenote where Jaime shares details of Mayan culture with us and points out different rock formations. Dani, armed with her waterproof case, documents the journey, careful not to interrupt Jaime while he's teaching. The water is freezing cold, my breathing slows the further we go, but I feel a gentle pressure on my back beneath the surface and without looking I know it's Rome. My body recognizes the bliss Rome's hands bring to it. His touch scorches my skin, leaving an imprint of him in its wake.

"You good?" He asks, low enough for only my ears.

I steady my breathing before answering him. I can't let him know the effect he has on me. We can't go back. No matter how much my body yearns for his touch. "I'm okay."

He hums his agreement, but he doesn't move his hand from my back for the rest of the tour, keeping the cold temperatures at bay.

We exit out of the Cenote to find an oasis waiting for us. The crystal blue waters look up to a

cylindrical rock wall about thirty feet tall. Different types of flora cover portions of the structure, making parts of the cenote appear shrouded in darkness while others appear to be bathed in the light of the sun.

We climb to the top where there's a pier that hangs off the edge. From here, the water looks to be different shades of blue. Some of the plants have fallen into the water, forming a border around certain parts.

Jaime informs us we can jump off the pier and the rocks if we desire but makes it clear that it's completely optional.

"I'ma sit this one out," Dani announces, pulling her phone back out to record more footage.

Ri and Arnold break off to take in more of the rock formations while Cortez runs off in search of the highest rock to jump from.

"I'm jumping. Who's with me?" Evie looks around the remaining crowd.

"I'm sorry but I gotta ask, you sure you're good with this, Eve?"

"Yeah. Why do you ask?"

"You had to take medication to get on a plane but you're willing to jump off a cliff?" Rome asks, dumbfounded.

She shrugs. "Don't question the process, Rome. I'm a thrill seeker. Planes are just necessary evil death traps."

Jalen chortles at that, completely enraptured by all that is Evie.

Micah nods his head with a smile. "She's got a point."

Rome lets out a laugh and holds his hands up in surrender. "Yes ma'am."

Micah and Troy head off to find the spots they want to jump from, while Evie takes her position on the pier and Jalen follows her.

Cortez, finally having found the highest point, announces his jump and does a backflip into the water, screaming like a bitch the whole way down. He receives a lackluster round of applause before Micah jumps next.

I look around, in awe of where we've ended up. "This is absolutely beautiful," I sigh.

"Yeah, it is." When I peer over at Rome, expecting to find him watching the scenery in front of us, I find him watching me instead.

"Rome," I groan. When he looks at me like that, he makes me want things I can't have. He makes me want it all.

"Just making an observation, J. That's all."

Needing to break away from the trance his stare has me in, I look away to catch my bearings. "Are you gonna jump?"

"Yep. The real question is, are you?"

"What do you mean by that?"

"Taking a leap doesn't scare me, J. I'm just waiting to see where you stand on that."

I glance between him and the water, knowing he's not talking about cliff jumping but not knowing how to answer his question. "What if taking a leap terrifies me?"

Because it does. Rome terrifies me. Yes, the idea of Ri and my mom finding out and twisting the bond we shared into something ugly picks at my brain constantly, but the real fear? The real fear is Rome himself. His dick has already branded my pussy making her useless to anyone else, including my damn self, and it's only been a week. If we keep going, I'm bound to catch feelings and then what? We try to make it work in the real world where we barely have time to breathe as it is? I have too much going on, too much I'm working toward to be able to afford the inevitable heartbreak Rome will bring me.

"My advice? Do it anyway."

"That's it? That's your profound advice? If something scares you, do it anyway?"

"Yep. If you don't do things that scare you, how can you say you've really lived? Me personally? I want to look back on my life and know I was brave enough to do the things that brought me joy despite the risks, even if they didn't work out."

Here he goes, making me question every decision I've ever made. My thoughts drift to Labor of Love. I've spent over a year just thinking about making a move on it and yet I still haven't. Why? Because if I fail, I will not only have let myself down, but tons of Black women in need. Sharing the expansion part of the idea with Rome gave it wings and yet the idea of going for it still makes me cower in fear.

"Jump with me, J." He holds his hand out to me, waiting patiently.

I can't answer him about the leap he really wants me to take right now, but I can give him this. I grab his hand and we back up to get a running start, diving into the waiting waters.

When we come up for air, Rome moves toward me with a determined gleam in his eye. I panic under his scrutiny, dipping my head under the water and holding my breath until my lungs constrict. When I break the surface, Rome's nowhere to be found.

Rome's words have haunted me since we left the tour, sticking to me like glue and infecting my every thought.

He kept his distance from me for the ATV ride back and I didn't see him again until the group dinner. He excused himself to his room after, not interested in small talk with anyone.

We could very well spend the rest of this vacation together and then completely cut ties. We could attempt some semblance of dating after this, and it could all fall apart. But even if that happens, is that a reason to not enjoy each other while we can?

We get each other and we make each other feel good. I'm over here going through phantom orgasms and for what?

The answer that was so solid in my mind before is now muddy and unfocused.

I pull Evie to the side, wanting to unburden myself to the person I trust the most. "I need to tell you something."

Her eyes practically jump out of her head. "Tell me, tell me."

"I was sleeping with Rome for most of this trip."

Her lids sink and her lips turn to a scowl. "Oh. I didn't know we were filming another episode of Things I Already Know, but okay. So?"

What the fuck? "What do you mean things you already know? How could you possibly have known?"

She crosses her arms. "Because I'm not a dumbass? Y'all have been giving off we're fucking vibes from the very beginning."

"If that were true, how come everyone else doesn't know?" Aside from Micah, but I don't need to share that with her right now.

"I'm the only one paying attention, I guess. Also, I saw you come out of his room one night."

"Evie! You could've told me that."

She shrugs. "I was letting you live your best life. But trust and believe if you hadn't told me the moment we got back home I would've pressed your ass. My question is why did you say was like past tense?"

I fill her in on the arrangement we made and how it came to an end. She seems completely unaffected by my story, not bothering to ask any questions along the way.

"Well?" I urge, once finished.

"Well what?"

"Don't you have anything to say?"

"I mean, what do you want me to say?"

"I don't know what I want you to say. I just want you to say what you wanna say."

She folds her arms across her chest. "You're really bad at this game. Okay follow up question. Why are you telling me about this now?"

"Because I couldn't hold it in anymore," I offer.

"So, what is it you want from me?"

I sigh. "To tell me I made the right decision."

She scoffs. "Or, maybe because you know me better than that, you want me to tell you to woman the fuck up and go for what you want. And maybe you're wanting me to help cover for you since there are a lot more wandering eyes around now."

I take a deep breath. I both hate and love when she reads me for filth. "Maybe."

"Well, are you waiting for me to say it again? I don't do encores for free."

I suck my teeth, rolling my eyes. "Yeah yeah, I heard you."

"And yet you're still standing here with me instead of going to hop on that grade A dick."

"Are you rushing me so you can go hop on the other Martin brother's dick? Don't think I didn't notice the vibes y'all were giving off earlier. I thought you didn't mess with guys with kids?"

She taps her foot in annoyance. "There were no vibes."

"There were vibes."

She taps her foot again. "No vibes."

"There were vibes. You wanna know how I know?"

"How?"

"You didn't even acknowledge what I said about you not dating guys with kids."

She heaves out an exhausted breath. Evie normally has a better poker face than this, which is how I know Jalen has her flustered. She can deny it all she wants but apparently these Martin brothers have a way of luring you into your web and holding on for dear life. "Well, the man is six-foot-nine so it's a little hard to see the red flags all the way up there, you know?

"I do know. So, you admit there were vibes."

"There weren't any damn vibes."

"Mhm, so he's not the reason you stopped trying to climb Micah like a tree?"

"No, I stopped trying to climb Micah because I've also been paying attention to the vibes he and Dani are giving off. I may be a hoe but I'm a loyal hoe so that's dead. Now, I love you, but I'm over you. Go get your man and leave the rest of the rest of us dickless bitches in peace."

So, I'm not the only one who noticed something up with those two. What the hell is happening to me and my girls? We cannot all go out like this.

Not wanting to waste another moment away from Rome, I chalk it up to my new motto—what happens in Tulum, stays in Tulum.

I wave goodbye to Evie and run to his room.

After I knock, he answers in a pair of sweats and no shirt. He takes in my blue floral bodycon dress with fire in his gaze. No words are exchanged as he steps aside to let me in. They aren't needed. We let our bodies do the talking.

CHAPTER TEN

Rome

"**T**HIS SHIT IS SO FUCKING GOOD," JANELLE MOANS, HER CADENCE thrown off by the smacking of my hips against her ass. She sucks in a breath, exhaling harshly.

We've been going nonstop since she showed up at my door late last night. We'd only gone one day without me being inside of her, and it was enough to have us ravenous for each other when we finally reconnected.

We got up, brushed our teeth, and showered with the intention of starting our day but somehow, we ended up back in this bed with her face down, ass up.

"I should punish you for trying to keep this good pussy away from me, J."

Her walls grip me tight at that declaration, pulling a groan from the depths of my stomach. This woman is a damn succubus.

"Oh, fuck. Yeah, punish me, Rome. I deserve it."

I push her down, forcing the arch in her back to deepen so far that her face sinks into the mattress. I grab her leg and hike it up to meet my waist, plunging deeper into her pussy. She lets out a string of words that sound more like gibberish as I pound into her. I grip a handful of her ass, kneading it firmly, but when she surges her hips forward, trying to run from me, I let go of her ass to pin her back in place.

"Nah, don't run. You wanted this, J. You deserve it, right?" Another slew of gibberish. I fold my body over hers to trail kisses down her spine. "You like how I punish you, J?"

"Yessss," she screams.

"You gonna keep this pussy from me again?"

"Noooo," she moans, her mouth full of bedsheets.

"This mine, J?" I ask, lifting her leg higher.

"Yes!"

"Say that shit." She whimpers in response, yanking on the sheets with a death grip. "I can't let you come 'til you give me the words, baby."

She plants her palms on the bed and using her wobbly arms, she lifts her head up. "It's yours, Rome. All yours."

Her words wash over me, giving me the strength of a thousand soldiers. With a sinister smile on my face, I lower her leg and reach my hand around to rub her clit. Her clit hardens under my touch and her breathing accelerates with her impending orgasm. Soon, I feel the familiar sensation of her milking me completely as she shouts my name.

"You think you've been punished enough, J?"

"Mmm, yes," she groans, completely out of breath.

I shake my head, tightening my grip on her before I lower myself onto my side on the bed. I never break our connection; I simply lift her leg on top of mine so I can keep stroking her deeply. "Nah, I don't think so."

"Rome," she cries.

"Yeah, keep saying that shit. I love how you say my name, J."

"Rome, you fucking demon, ooh fuck," her voice runs out of steam as I stroke her into oblivion.

"You always talking all that good shit, J." I run my hands along her stomach, up to cup her breasts. I'll never get tired of the way her body feels. The way her breasts fit perfectly in my hands, the soft feel of her stomach, the smooth expanse of her thighs.

I can't walk away from this woman.

I hear her swallow a gulp of air as she steadies herself to start throwing her ass back at me. "Because I can back it up."

"Oh yeah? Come on this dick then. Since you can back it up."

She throws her arm out to catch herself when I meet her thrust. She sucks in a breath and lets it out to say, "You know the rules, Rome. Make me."

"Bet."

With that, I push her leg off me and straddle her hips to plow into her. Any other words she has to say die on her throat, melting into nothing more than whimpers.

It doesn't take long for her to clench around me again and the euphoric feeling of her release coats me. I follow her over the edge, emptying inside of her.

She stretches her leg out, groaning as I turn her over and pull her to my side.

"Remember when I said there were more humane ways to kill me? That was one of them," she yawns.

I chuckle, moving one of her braids out of her face. "I'll remember that going forward." I expect her to recoil at any mention of the future but she's so languid in my arms right now, I don't even know if she heard me.

"Why did we even bother showering? I'm sweaty all over again."

"I'm pretty sure you mauled me so it's your own fault," I taunt.

"I mauled you? If that's true, then I was just trying to get back at you, Caveman. I will send you the bill for my damn chain and my dress." She points her finger at my face as she scolds me.

When she showed up at my door, looking like a vixen in that skin tight dress with the silver thigh chain peeking out from under it, I couldn't wait to get my hands on her. I may have busted the zipper of her dress in my hurry, and I may have torn the chain straight off her leg.

I wrap my hand around her finger and kiss the tip of it. "I'll buy you all the dresses and thigh chains you want."

"Mhm, you think I'm playing. I get all my chains and beads custom made by a woman who makes them for the thickies of the world and she only sells them in sets."

She tries to appear menacing but, honestly, she's never looked cuter. I resist telling her that though because telling her she looks cute when she's mad will no doubt transform her into full on terrifying.

"What's her info? I'll buy her whole inventory right now." I grab my phone prepared to look her up, but Janelle pushes my hand down.

"You do know that buying me a whole new collection of body jewelry doesn't give you the right to continuously rip them off me, right?"

"Debatable."

"Rome!" She playfully slaps my arm.

"Listen, you need to own your part here," I laugh. "I was prepared to be on my Olivia Pope 'you want me, earn me' shit after you played games at the cenote, but you showed up looking too damn tempting."

She buries her head into my chest, giggling. "Now I'm wishing I had changed into some baggy sweats or something before coming over. I would pay good money to hear you give me the 'you want me, earn me' speech."

"Make no mistake, J, no matter what you wore over here it was getting ripped off. I had just planned on giving you shit first."

"Fair. I have been a little difficult the past few days."

"It's all good. You came to your senses eventually."

"Wow. So humble."

"What do I need to be humble for? It's a simple fact. I want to spend my vacation using every faculty on my body to bring you back-to-back toe-curling orgasms and I know you want that too. What reason do I have to deny or downplay it?"

She agrees but murmurs something about not needing to be so loud about being right, prompting a laugh out of me.

We finally pull ourselves out of the bed to get started with our day. While she takes a second shower, I wash up at the sink and come back out to change.

As I finish applying my favorite beard oil, she comes out of the bathroom wearing nothing but a towel. I ask the ancestors for the willpower to not rip it away from her right now.

"Don't even think about it. I'm not taking another shower. I'm already gonna be late because I need to go back to my room to change," Janelle says with her back to me.

"You don't even know what I was thinking," I joke.

She spins around, frowning. "Mmm, I don't? Now who's tryna downplay shit?"

"Touché. What are you gonna be late for anyway?"

"I'm going to meet Nova."

"Nova is the infamous Wheezie's daughter, right?" I remember meeting her at last night's dinner. I also remember Amerie making a show of telling her in front of everyone how she added a pink ribbon to her bouquet in Wheezie's honor and Nova looking put off by the gesture.

"Yeah, that's her. She's my favorite cousin even though my cousin, Mina, swears that spot is hers."

"Did I meet Cousin Mina?"

"Yeah, she was the one with the corkscrew mohawk."

"That's right. Okay, cool. So, what are you and Nova getting into today?" I'm spending the afternoon with Jalen, but I wouldn't mind running into Janelle. My inability to get enough of her is just sad at this point.

"I have no idea but knowing Nova, nothing but trouble." She smiles at me, slipping into a pair of my shorts and a t-shirt. "See how ridiculous I look? All because you couldn't take two seconds to unzip my dress." She holds her hands out at her sides, spinning around to show me how my clothes fit her. They're not baggy to the point where they look like she's swimming in them but they're far looser than she prefers.

"You could never look ridiculous." I walk up to her, kissing her on the forehead.

"Alright, now. You done already got the drawers so you ain't got to lie, Craig."

I smack her on the ass. "Simple ass, weren't you gonna be late?"

"Oooh, now he's rushing me. I see how it is. Fine, I'm gone. Are you doing ziplining later?"

"Why? You gonna miss me?"

She puts the palm of her hand against my forehead and pushes. "Bye, Rome."

I grab her by the waist. "I'm playing, I already know you will. Yes, I'll be there later."

She struggles in my hold but then gives up and leans into me. "Good, if you're nice I'll let you stand behind me in line so you can watch my ass when I go down the zipline."

"Hilarious that you thought anybody but me would be standing behind you." I can; however, think of one person who would try to take my spot. I've never liked Arnold's cousin, Cortez. He thinks far too highly of himself.

He puts too much stock in the fact that he's Marquise Hightower's nephew. I don't think he's ever even watched any of Marquise's games, let alone picked up a football himself. Everything he does is for clout. He lives off his parent's money but acts like he's God's gift to women. Watching him press up on Janelle the way he did only deepened my hatred. He hit on both Dani and Evie during the tour yesterday, and then went after all of Amerie's friends last night at dinner. He always circled back around to Janelle though. "I think Cortez is in our group for the day again, though. Are you good with that?"

She turns in my arms to face me. "I find it very interesting that you chose to ask me about Cortez instead of Troy."

"Why would I be concerned about Troy? I know my girl is faithful to me."

"You are not referring to my pussy as your girl again."

"We go together forreal. I told you to ask her and she'll tell you. I'm not worried about Troy, but if someone is making you uncomfortable, that's when I have a problem."

She loops her arms behind my shoulders. "So that Caveman act is good for something, huh? Cortez isn't a problem. He's obnoxious but nothing I can't handle."

"And you'll tell me if that changes?"

"Of course."

With that, she gives me a quick kiss then peeks her head out of my room before making a mad dash for her own.

About thirty minutes later, I meet Jalen out front so we can head into town. Our concierge, Javier, told us about a cigar bar that features live music at night but is open during the day as well, so we're headed there.

When we get there, we pay extra to have a private section. A few people recognize Jalen, but no one approaches him so he relaxes a bit more.

"You checked in with Killa Kam today?" I ask him.

"Yeah. Dad had him watching *Annabelle* last night. He said when he woke up, he was convinced one of his Funko Pop figures moved so he threw it out. Then his ass gonna have the nerve to ask me if I can replace it because he really liked that one. I told him go ask Pops."

"Ayo, that's wild. Where was Mom at?"

He gives me a look that says to be serious. "Sleep."

"For someone who says she be shutting shit down on all her girls' trips, she can't ever stay up past nine at home."

"I'm saying."

We share a laugh, both of us taking a puff of our cigars. "What else is going on? How's Tiff?"

Last I checked, things were running smoothly with his ex-wife, but things can change at the drop of a hat with her.

Jalen runs his hand down his face, sighing deeply. "She's working the few nerves I have, bruh."

"What's up now? Everything was fine two weeks ago."

"And then she found out I was coming to this wedding, and she started bugging. I almost didn't make it because she kept saying if she couldn't come to the wedding, she didn't understand why she couldn't keep Kam for the week. Alone."

Tiffany and Jalen's custody agreement is that Jalen has Kam full-time while Tiffany is allowed supervised visitation. She has yet to prove she can handle keeping him by herself, so I understand why he freaked out.

"I know Mom wasn't having that, though."

"Sure wasn't. She told Tiff if she tried to pull up to their house to get Kam, she was gonna get introduced to Claudette."

Claudette is the taser our mom keeps in the house. She replaces it every two years, but she always names it Claudette for some reason. I met Claudette once in high school when I was sneaking back into the house late and our mom thought I had broken in. She's not to be fucked with; the taser nor my mom.

"Damn, I know she ran scared after that."

"Haven't heard from her since."

A different waitress comes in with the drinks we ordered. She looks a bit too young to be working here but she looks a little stunned to see Jalen. To her credit, she tries her best to keep her composure when asking if we need anything else, but she can't stop staring at him. Finally, she caves and asks him for a picture which he happily obliges.

We pass the time with cigars and drinks. He tells me that Kam is interested in playing basketball at school next year and I fill him in on my latest work deal.

"So, what's up with you and Miss Janelle? Things didn't look great at dinner last night, you in trouble?"

"Why you assume I'm the problem?"

"Why not?"

"Damn. It be your own people."

"What you do?"

I tell him about the past week with Janelle and how it's supposed to be a vacation fling but that I want more once we leave.

"Right, because she's sis-in-law."

"Bruh, stop saying that. No one is getting married besides Arnold and Amerie."

"Yet."

"Man. Enough outta you."

"Okay, bet. But this little conversation is going in my best man toast at your wedding."

"Can we focus on the now?"

"Have you told her that you're tryna date her once we get home?"

"Of course not. I just got her to stop running from me for the rest of the vacation. Can't do too much too soon."

"I mean, if you pussy just say that."

I chuckle around my cigar. "That's nuts."

"Or lack thereof."

"Jalen, stop playin with me."

He snorts, taking another pull from his cigar. "Aight, I'm done. I will reserve any further commentary for my toast."

"Fuck outta here."

Later that day, ziplining goes by without too many issues. Arnold switched up the group that was supposed to go, claiming to have needed a break from Amerie and her nagging. The two of them were supposed to do some sort of dance lesson with his parents, her parents, and Arnold's aunt and uncle, but he convinced her to take a few of the girls at the spa instead. He and his dad joined us for ziplining along with Christian and a few others.

Cortez was on his bullshit, hyper focusing on Janelle the whole day, but Marquise distracted him enough times and I stayed close by.

Luckily, we have the rest of the night to ourselves. I plan to shower and find Janelle, but when I round the corner of the hotel, I hear Janelle getting into it with her mom.

"Ma, what is the problem? I don't understand."

"I just don't see why you didn't go to the spa with us today. Your sister was visibly upset and she could've used some moral support from you. Do you think it was appropriate for you to spend your afternoon with Arnold? Sometimes I wonder if you purposefully make things harder for yourself."

I'm shocked by the sharpness in her mother's voice. She and Amerie seem determined to bring Janelle down, and it's working. Janelle's shoulders deflate. She struggles to find her words.

"Why are you acting like I went out on a date with the man? It was a group activity with him and fourteen other people. He's about to be my brother-in-law and you're acting like it's taboo for me to be in the same room with him. That's just weird. And as far as Ri being upset, she didn't want me to come to the spa day so what was I supposed to do? Beg her?"

Her mom sighs disappointedly. "I did not raise you to be selfish, Janelle."

"Excuse me?"

"And Amie tells me she tried to set you up with a nice gentleman here and you rebuffed her offer."

"Are you serious right now?"

"Dead serious. You can't spend your entire life pretending you don't need people, Janelle."

I've heard enough. I continue rounding the corner, heading straight for Janelle and her mom. "Hi Janelle, Mrs. Cross. Apologies, Deb."

She smiles brightly at me. "Well, hello Rome. Were you part of the ziplining group today?" Her tone drips with disdain at the mention of ziplining.

"I sure was. We had a good time. It was so nice of Amerie to insist Janelle do it, because she's been working so hard on the wedding. I'm sure she needed a break."

Her mom looks utterly confused at my statement. "Ah, yes, well the engagement party was wonderful."

I barely contain my disgust. It figures Amerie told her mom everything but the good things.

"Oh, no. I mean this past week. There's been a lot of last minute adjustments and Janelle's been handling them like a champ."

She looks back at Janelle with raised brows. "Really?"

"Yep. She ran around searching for that pink ribbon for Wheezie." I rattle off a few other errands Janelle has been charged with since being here. "Amerie even lost her ring the other day and Janelle was instrumental in finding it."

She gasps with her hand on her chest. "She lost her ring?!"

"Yes ma'am. She had us all worried sick, but it all worked out."

"I can't believe that girl, so irresponsible. I gotta go see her. Okay, thank you sweetie. Have a great night. Janelle, I will see you later." She hurries off before either of us can respond.

Janelle nudges me with her elbow. "You did not have to snitch on her for the ring," she snickers.

"I absolutely did. You okay?"

"How much did you hear?"

"Enough."

"Then no. But I will be. I'm used to this by now."

"Doesn't make it okay, J. Come on."

"Where we going?"

"Where do you wanna go?"

"My room."

"Then that's where we're going."

I follow her to her room without pretense. There's no checking over our shoulders to see if anyone's watching. There's no waiting fifteen minutes before heading to her room. We're just two people enjoying each other's company, not giving a fuck what anyone has to say about it.

CHAPTER ELEVEN

Janelle

I LATCH MY HANDS TOGETHER, HOPING THAT WILL STOP THEM FROM fidgeting. The shaking in my hands stops but my knee starts bouncing in their place, rattling the table in the restaurant where I'm waiting for my parents.

I could've done this lunch with just my mom, but I wanted my dad to pay witness to it so there was no chance my mom could misconstrue the story to him later. This conversation with her is long overdue and after the way she spoke to me yesterday, it can't wait a second longer.

My mom and dad step into the hotel restaurant, scanning the crowd for me. My dad sends me one of his megawatt smiles when he sees me waving them over. I can't bring myself to look at my mom just yet.

"Hi, my nugget. You look beautiful." He engulfs me in one of those bear hugs he's famous for and I melt into it, needing all the warmth I can get.

"Hi, Daddy. Thank you."

"I wasn't expecting your invite today, Janelle. Everything okay?" My mom asks as she sits down. Leave it up to her to jump right in.

Let's do this.

"Actually, no. Everything's not okay."

She perks up in surprise, shifting her body closer to me. "What's wrong, baby? Tell your mama how she can help."

"I'm glad you're feeling so helpful because my issue is with you."

She gasps while my dad doesn't look all that surprised to hear these words from me. He knows I've been toeing the line with his wife for as long as I can remember. "With me? How so?"

"Mom, what kind of daughter do you think I am?"

Our server arrives at that moment to take our drink orders. I want nothing more than to order a neat tequila but I want to stay clear headed for this conversation, so I opt to stick with water.

The moment our server walks away my mom lasers in on me. "What kind of question is that?"

"One I'd like you to answer."

She lifts her hands in exasperation, but I remain still, not willing to give an inch. The moment I do, she'll pounce. "Well, I don't know how I'm supposed to answer that."

"Okay, well yesterday you told me that you didn't raise me to be selfish, but you also didn't raise me to be the type of daughter who would make a move on my sister's fiancé and yet that's exactly how you treated me."

"Wait, what? Run that by me again," my dad interrupts.

My mom ignores him and presses on. "Sweetie, I wasn't implying that you would do that."

My face remains deadpan while I ignore my mom and turn to my dad. "Your wife implied I was a whore who can't be trusted around Arnold because he's so irresistible I must want to hop on his dick at any moment."

"Janelle," my mom reprimands. "That is not what I said."

"Do you think it was appropriate for you to spend the afternoon with Arnold?" I throw her words back at her. "What else was I supposed to take from that?"

"It's just that emotions run high during events like this. It's easy to get caught up and make mistakes."

"Mistakes? Mistakes like what?"

"Mistakes like...I don't know, just mistakes. I'm just looking out for you, sweetie. I know this wedding is hard for you."

I am so tired of hearing that. "No. It's not hard at all. If you ever stopped to listen to a word I say you would know that I could not care less about this wedding. I'm happy for Ri. I'm happy for Arnold. I don't have any lingering feelings for him, and I don't appreciate you gaslighting me about that. Let's not forget who dated Arnold first, so if you want to talk to someone not being the woman you raised, I think you're talking to the wrong daughter."

"There's no need to be nasty toward your sister."

"Deb, mmmm mmm." My dad shakes his head at my mom. He doesn't get involved often, preferring to let us work out our problems on our own and offer his own support separately; so when he does get involved my mom knows she's bordering on the point of no return.

She clears her throat. "That wasn't my intention."

"Forgive me if I don't believe you, Mom. I don't know what I did to make you think so low of me but I'm at the point where I don't care what you or Ri think. I don't have anything to prove to you. Your issues with me are not my problem."

She takes my hand in hers over the table. "No, no. I'm sorry, I'm so sorry. This isn't what I wanted."

Our server brings out our drinks, giving me an opportunity to break the physical connection between me and my mom. A mother's touch is supposed to be calming and soothing, but my mother's touch feels suffocating. I feel myself choking on her expectations and perceptions.

I tell our server that I need more time to think about my order so she excuses herself. Truthfully, I haven't even looked at the menu. I don't even think we'll be eating at this rate because I'm ready to walk out.

"Where was I?" she questions.

"You weren't really saying much of anything."

"I'm trying to explain here."

"Are you?"

She slams her hand on the table, drawing the eyes of others around us. "Damnit, Janelle. You have never needed me."

"What are you talking about?"

"Ever since you were a kid you never needed me for anything. It was either your dad or no one. You taught yourself how to tie your shoes. Your dad taught you how to ride a bike. You worked through boy issues on your own. Your dad taught you how to drive. You killed undergrad without so much as a complaint. I never heard a peep from you during medical school. You just never relied on me. When everything happened with you, Amerie, and Arnold, I just knew you would need me. I just knew something like this would eat you up inside and you'd finally need me to get you through something. I guess I convinced myself that was the truth even when you said it wasn't."

My head spins at this revelation. Confusion gives way to rage as I take in my mother's earnest smile. As if her confession will automatically fix decades of issues between us. She turns her palm up on the table, expecting me to join hands with her. Fuck that.

"That…that doesn't even make sense."

Her smile falters. I can still feel the warmth her hand left on mine but the gap between us grows even wider. "What?"

"Did you think that was supposed to make it all better? What daughter doesn't need her mother? I always needed you, but I never wanted to be a burden to you because you were always wrapped up in what Ri needed. I never hated you or her for that it just was what it was, but your solution for our lack of a bond was to make me feel less than just so I would finally lean on you? And then you sit here and you say that with your whole chest like it's okay and you think I'm gonna forgive you just like that?" She's got me fucked up if she thinks we're about to hug it out like a happy family.

A tear pools in the corner of her eye, but she dabs it with a napkin before it can fall. My dad rubs circles on her back but grabs my hand under the table. I appreciate him for being able to remain neutral. I don't expect him to leave his wife out to dry when she's crying in the middle of a restaurant, but I do need to feel heard by at least one parent right now and as always, he delivers.

My mom chokes out a sob as she tries to get her next words out. "Baby girl. I am so sorry. I've gone about this all wrong."

"Umm, hi. I'm sorry but are you ready to place your order?" Our server says, startling all of us. She looks uncomfortable, knowing she's interrupted a tense moment. My mom swipes at her eyes, trying her best to hide her tears.

"That's okay. I'm actually not staying." I declare. I have to get out of here before the weight of my mom's betrayal fully hits me. For years, I wondered why my mom thought less of me. Why I could never do anything right in her eyes, but in actuality she was just willing to rip my confidence to shreds to make herself feel better about not being there for me the way she should've when I was a kid.

My mom tries to protest my leaving, but I nod at our server and she takes the opportunity to run from our table.

"You don't have to leave, Janelle. We can sit and talk through this."

"I really don't want to, Mom. You've had a lifetime to sit and talk to me. I appreciate you finally telling me the truth, but I've heard enough."

"What does that even mean?" Her voice comes out in a shrill way. "I'm still your mother and we still have the wedding to go to."

"That's what everything comes back around to. What Amerie needs."

"It's not that. She's just always needed me more than you did."

"Therefore making her more valuable as a daughter, right? You know what's worse? I'm no better. I coddle Ri just as much as you because that's all I've ever known. I always put her feelings before my own, because that's all I ever saw from you growing up."

She has no argument because she knows it's true. Rome was right about needing to be willing to put myself first. I don't want to make any big decisions about my relationship with my mom while on a beach in Mexico but for once, I'm not going to force myself to someone else's timeline. "When I'm ready to talk again, I'll let you know," I say, standing from the table.

"Janelle…"

"Please, just listen to me for once."

She tearfully nods and leans her head against my dad's shoulder. I stand from the table, bending to kiss my dad on his bald head and then I walk out with my head held high.

As I'm walking back to my room, I check my phone and see a message from Rome.

Rome: Let me know how it goes

I told him I was going to be confronting my mom today and he offered to come along but I wanted to do it alone, so I promised to fill him in later.

Me: It's over—Not sure if I'm still gonna have a relationship with my mom when I get home but I said what I needed to say

Rome: It's over already? Did you even eat?

Me: No. Lost my appetite after that

Rome: I'm sorry. Need me to come over?

Me: Nope I'm taking a long bath and I'm sleeping til it's time to go out tonight. Thank you though *kissy emoji*

Rome: Sleep well, J

I plan to. Tonight we are having the bachelor and bachelorette parties for Arnold and Ri. The men are going to a nighttime pool bar and hookah lounge and the women are going to a dance club. I need to get all the rest I can get to be prepared to socialize tonight. By the time I see Ri tonight I'm sure our mom will have told her about our conversation so she may be expecting me to confront her as well. It's well past time we had a talk but because old habits die hard I'm willing to grin and bear it until the wedding is over.

Twenty minutes later, there's a knock at my door. I open it to find Javier and another concierge who push two carts into my room. The first cart is packed with lunch consisting of tostadas and elote; different desserts including sopaipillas, tres leches, and chocolate covered strawberries; a bottle of white wine on ice; and a glass of Mezcalita. The second cart is filled with self-care essentials from bath bombs and salts to body creams, massage oils, a candle, and a sleep mask.

Javier hands me a note to accompany the goodies, giving me a knowing smile. He protests when I give him a tip because whoever had the items sent already tipped him, but I insist.

I'm proud of you. -RM

My teeth sink into my bottom lip as I look over all the things he sent for me. How is it that I've owned bras for longer than I've known this man but he's so in tune with exactly what I need? And to think, I almost let him slip through my fingers. I won't do that again.

I pull out my phone and snap a picture of myself with one of the tostadas raised to my lips, the food cart in front of me. I send it to Rome with a message.

> Me: You wanna be a book boyfriend so bad

> Rome: I wanna be a two-dimensional man who doesn't even exist? Pass

> Me: See all that hater energy? A book boyfriend would never

> Rome: Put my girlfriend on the phone she talks to me nice

> Me: Me: *eye roll emoji* She's busy

> Rome: *eye emoji* Without me!? *insert Soulja Boy meme*

> Me: Omg thanks for the goodies Rome byeeeeeeee

> Rome: Wowwwwww

> Rome: Essence would never

The sound of banging on my door jolts me out of my sleep. I check my phone to see that I had five more minutes on my alarm until I needed to meet the ladies in Dani's room. Whoever cost me five minutes of sleep better be dying.

I open my door to find an alive and well Arnold. He's dressed for the evening in his gray and white plaid linen pants with a black muscle fit knitted t-shirt tucked into it. He's fitted with his signature Patek watch, his single gold hoop earring, and the gaudy ass ring I hate that he wears to every special occasion. The thing is the size of a championship ring and every time someone asks him about it, he feels the need to regale them of the story of how he bought it for himself to celebrate his own championship of opening his agency.

"What's up, Arnold?"

He stumbles over his own feet, using the door jamb to catch himself. I may have spoken too soon about him being both alive and well. One look at his red rimmed eyes lets me know he's far from sober.

"Heyyyy, Ellie-Elle." I cringe at the nickname he always used for me whenever he was drunk. I know when that nickname comes out that he's fucked up. He once repeated the name to himself thirty times in a row because he was so tickled by it.

"Pre-gamed a little too hard, huh?"

The force of his laughter tips him over and I throw my hand out to help balance him. "Ha, I've been drinking since ten a.m."

I peek out into the hallway, trying to see if any of the guys are walking by so they can help him get to where he needs to go. If Ri sees him like this, there's bound to be a fight.

"Well, good for you. Did you need something?"

Confident that he's steady on his feet, I move my hand from his arm, but he grabs it with a vice grip. "I need to talk to you."

I shake free of his grip and back away to grab a water bottle from the dresser. His eyes track my every movement until I'm standing in front of him again. "Okay, why don't you have some water and then we can talk." I try to step around him outside of my room so we can talk in the hallway, but he holds firm to the door. He's so unsteady on his feet I can't tell if he intentionally blocked my path or if the door is the only thing keeping him up.

He takes a swig of water, letting some of it drip down his chin, and blinks a few times. "I drank it. We can talk now?" He holds the bottle out to me, but I wave my hand to tell him to keep it.

"What do you wanna talk about? You should probably be going to sober up so Ri doesn't see you out like this."

He blows out a raspberry. "Psh, Ri's always nagging about something."

He's not wrong but I'm not about to sit here and co-sign on shit talk about my sister from her man. "She just worries about you. You've got a long night ahead of you and you're already sauced."

"She ain't worried bout me. She just wants to show you up." I freeze in place. I can't take anymore revelations about how my family feels about me today. Whatever issues Ri has with me, I want to hear them from her and her only. Arnold laughs to himself, dropping the hand holding the water and I subtly tip the bottle up, keeping it from spilling on the floor. "You wouldn't nag me. You never nagged me when we were together."

His eyes roam my face, landing on my lips. *Oh fuck.* My alarm goes off on my phone, piercing Arnold's concentration long enough to give me a reprieve from his intense gaze. "Maybe you should go find Ri and talk to her if you're upset."

He takes a step toward me, holding his hands out in front of him for balance. "Mmm mmm, I don't wanna talk to Ri. I wanna talk to you."

"Arnold, go sober up and get your shit together before you do something you regret." I don't want to have to break Arnold's jaw before his wedding, but I will. I glance over at my phone, wondering if I can grab it without him stepping any closer to me.

"The only regret I have is you losing. Is you. Is losing," he clears his throat and blinks back into focus. "Is losing you. I made a mistake. I chose the wrong sister."

Good lord. I just scolded my mom for implying anything would happen between Arnold and me and here this fool goes, saying dumb shit like this.

"Arnold, please shut up. I don't have time for this. Leave my room." I point behind him at the door, waiting for him to give in but he steps closer.

"Come on, Ellie-Elle. We were so good together." He takes another step closer, and I take two large steps back. He follows suit, crouching in on my space, so I back up again and reach for my phone. "You're so sexy. I wanna try again." He leans in to kiss me and I duck away from his hold.

"No! What is wrong with you?"

"Don't you mean what's right with me? I love you, Ellie-Elle."

"Fuck off, Arnold. I'm so serious. I'm trying my best not to beat your ass but you're making it hard."

He reaches for me again and I slap his arm. "You're making me hard. We can start over. Come on, baby."

"You can start over by yourself because when I tell Ri about this, it's over for you."

He rolls his eyes. "Please, you don't want that nag in your life either."

"You have one more time to call my sister a nag." He thinks I'm such a prize because I never nagged him during our relationship. The truth is, I never cared enough to nag him. We spent a year together and I emotionally checked out six months in. I didn't see a real future with him, so I didn't care what he was doing. I stayed in the relationship for as long as I did because I didn't want to lose him as a friend. Ri may be obnoxious and she and I have a whole host of issues to solve between us, but the love she has for Arnold is obvious. If he doesn't appreciate that, then he doesn't deserve her.

In my shocked haze, he manages to sneak up on me forcing me back as his lips descend on me. Before they connect, I bow my head and swing my arm, connecting my hand with his right cheek.

The slap reverberates through the room, echoing off the walls and shattering any illusions he might've had about what would happen when he came here tonight.

"Get the fuck out of my room. Now!" I give him a look that says 'try me again if you want to'. If he so much as breathes at me, I will take the past six months' worth of pent up aggression out on his face.

With his hand caressing his bruised cheek, he walks backwards sloppily toward the door, hauling ass down the hall once he reaches it.

I drop my head into my hands, letting out a small scream. This must be a joke. This can't possibly be how my life is going right now. Of course, my phone picks this very moment to ping with back-to-back messages from Evie and Dani asking where I am.

I already wasn't looking forward to tonight and now I'm fully dreading it.

When I get to Dani's room, I see that I'm the last to arrive. Despite the room being filled with fifteen other women, it somehow still looks organized. Dani has makeup stations set up in different corners of the room to keep everyone in their own spaces. She has two cameras set up: one in the corner to capture everyone's process and one directly in front of her so that she can record a Get Ready With Me video. Ri's station is set up directly next to hers because she'll be making an appearance in Dani's upcoming video.

I'm bombarded with hugs and kisses from my four cousins, including Nova and Mina. I'm overwhelmed by greetings from Ri's college friends, her cycling friends, one of the agents who works for Arnold, and a few other women I don't know. Dani tells me where to put my garment bag and leads me to my makeup station so I can join in on the festivities. Evie hands me a shot that I down in seconds.

Her brows furrow. "You good?"

I glance over at Ri, laughing with Dani and her college friend, Crystal. I can count on one hand the number of times I've seen Ri truly smile during this trip. My head is spinning, trying to find the right balance between what's right and what's best for everyone. The last thing I want to do is ruin a rare moment of happiness for Ri by telling her about Arnold, but I can't in good conscience let her walk down the aisle to him without her knowing.

"Uh, ask me again in five minutes." I march over to Ri and try to put as much pep into my voice as I can. "Hey, Ri, could I talk to you for a second?"

She peers up at me through her false lashes. Her makeup is stunning. Her eyeshadow is a bold orange and brown ombre that makes the chocolate of her eyes stand out. Her cheekbones are perfectly enhanced by the gold blush she's sporting and her lips are a glossy orange-reddish color, giving her a summer glow look.

She gets up without a fuss and joins me in the hallway outside of Dani's room.

"Listen, I don't know how to say this so…"

She puts her palm up, stopping my sentence short. "Hold up, if this is about you and Mom I really don't wanna hear it right now. Tonight is all about fun so let's just focus on that, okay?"

I wish our biggest problem was Mom right now. "No, it's not that."

"Nelly, you still gotta do your makeup and I wanna get dressed and get fucked up with my girls. Whatever you have to say can wait. I don't want any drama tonight. Can you do that for me?" I love how she says this like I'm the one causing the drama. I didn't ask for this shit to be brought to my door.

"I really think I should just tell you."

She plugs her ears with her fingers, singing to block me out. "No drama! Love you, bye!" she kisses me on the cheek and skips back into the room.

Great.

It only takes us forty-five minutes to get ready and another twenty to get to the club. We walk in as JayO's "22" is playing and Crystal, Nova, and Ri's other friend, Melinda run off to the dance floor. Ri intertwines our fingers and shimmies us through the crowd to join them. I try to let the music wash away my worries.

The guilt of not telling Ri about Arnold continues to needle my mind like a gnat so I drown it with alcohol. I've been throwing shots back like water since we got here. I'm not even sure how long we've been here, but I know I've heard about twenty different songs.

Evie pulls me off the dance floor to our now empty VIP section. "What's up? You don't get this drunk this quickly."

I dance by her side, whining my hips to the music. "What ol' boy say? I'm gonna dance my pain away, I got problems," I sing.

"You miss your man or something?" Evie pokes fun at me, bumping my hip with hers.

Maybe a dose of Rome is what I need right now but I don't want to interrupt his fun. My mind shifts to panic when I remember that he's with Arnold. What if he confesses what he did to Rome? Will Rome be upset that I didn't tell him first? Will Arnold spin it to seem like I came on to him? Matter of fact, what if he does the same thing with Ri and tells her what happened tonight but spins it in his favor?

Evie shoves a bottle of ice-cold water in my face and I chug the whole thing, ignoring the brain freeze. I tell her what happened with Arnold and her eyes widen in surprise.

"You have to tell her now."

"She didn't wanna hear it. She asked for a night of peace."

"Who gives a fuck? She hasn't given us a moment's peace since we landed."

"Damn, tell me how you really feel."

"Waiting is only gonna make it worse. She'll be more pissed that you didn't tell her immediately even though it's her fault you didn't. And I don't trust Arnold not to try to beat you to the punch."

She doesn't give me a chance to protest, grabbing my hand and dragging me to find Ri on the dance floor. Our cousins stare at us like we've lost our minds before tuning us out in favor of whatever song is playing now. I clutch Ri's hand and take her with me to the restrooms.

"What the hell is going on?" She asks, watching me check the stalls to see if we're alone.

"Arnold tried to kiss me," I blurt.

Her mouth falls open and I catch her right eye twitch slightly. "What did you say?"

"I said that Arnold tried to kiss me. I slapped him before it happened, but he did try."

"When?"

"Tonight. Right before I met up with you guys. He showed up to my room drunk, talking nonsense, and made a move." I know I should tell her the things he said too but she looks like she's about to go into shock from hearing about the kiss alone. I need to build up to that.

Ri braces her hands against the edge of the sink, dropping her head to her chest. She looks up and meets my eyes in the mirror, her face furious.

"I don't believe you."

Hold the fuck up. That is not at all how I thought she'd react. I thought there was a possibility she'd get mad at me because I'm the messenger, but I didn't think she wouldn't believe me.

"You don't believe me?"

"No."

"Why would I lie about this, Ri?"

"I don't know! You seem to want to ruin my wedding by any means necessary, but I didn't think you'd stoop this low."

"Ruin your wedding?" I screech. "I've been doing everything in my power to make this wedding perfect for you."

"If this is your idea of perfect, I feel bad for your patients."

I rear back as if slapped. She spins around leaning against the sink with her arms folded over her chest. "You know what it is?" She continues. "You're jealous."

"Jealous?" My heart starts racing making me dizzy. "The floor is yours, Amerie. Please explain how I'm jealous and what the fuck I'm jealous of."

"You're jealous of me. You're jealous of my relationship with Arnold. You're jealous of this wedding. You're jealous of my relationship with Mom. You want my life and I'm so sorry that you can't have it, but you can't. Arnold doesn't want you. He wouldn't try to kiss you so stop trying to come between us and just be happy for me!" She stomps her foot like a child.

"You sound so stupid right now."

"You're the one making up shit for attention."

I clasp my hands together in front of me. Warning bells go off in my head telling me to pull back, but I've allowed myself to be silenced for too long.

"No, you're the one too focused on me to even enjoy your own fucking wedding vacation. You've been up everyone's ass making everyone miserable because you're miserable. And even though you've treated me like shit the past two weeks, longer if I'm being real, I still defended you when your fiancé came to my room telling me he chose the wrong sister and how he wanted to run away with me. I came to you to try to save you some heartache, but you know what? You two clowns deserve each other. So fuck you, fuck him, fuck this whole fucking wedding."

Her breaths come out in harsh pants. She tries to process what's happening, but I can see it's killing her. She's fighting the truth I've given her, determined to twist it to work in her favor.

"You can't say fuck the wedding. You're the Maid of Honor."

I huff out a humorless laugh. That's what she took from everything I said? The optics of losing a member of her bridal party? She's delusional.

"Now's your chance to make Dani the Maid of Honor like you wanted, remember?"

"You're really gonna change your flight and leave?"

"Oh no, I'm not leaving. I'm gonna enjoy the last few days of my vacation, free from your bullshit. But you will not see me at that God damn wedding." I don't give a fuck that she and Arnold paid for everything. I won't even offer to pay them back for it. It's the least they can do for my pain and suffering. "I hope you two are very fucking happy together."

I snatch the door to the restroom open, running right into Dani. "Where the hell have you two been?! You don't have your phones?"

"Mine's in my pocket, why?"

"We have to go." Her voice is frantic. I immediately go on alert, preparing to hear terrible news.

"What happened?"

"Rome and the guys got into a bar fight!"

CHAPTER TWELVE

Rome

A few hours earlier

TAKE A SIP OF MY DRINK, THE AMBER LIQUID GOING DOWN SMOOTHLY. I survey the room with narrowed eyes, irritation prickling at my skin.

We've been at this bar for hours and I've been over it since hour one. Arnold showed up drunk as fuck, apparently having spent his day pre-gaming. He showed up with a bruise on his cheek and when I asked him what happened he said he slapped himself, trying to sober up, but forgot he had his ring on and cut himself.

Dumb as hell, but okay.

He's been rambling in circles about being a fuck up and needing to beg for something. Micah, Christian, and I tried to convince him to skip tonight since he clearly wasn't in a headspace where he could enjoy the night but he wouldn't hear it. I'm sure he's going to end up throwing up everywhere and we're going to have to hear Amerie's mouth about letting him get like this.

Every time I hand him some water to sober him up, Cortez sidles up to him to give him more liquor. To top it off, Cortez has some friends here that aren't invited to the wedding. When we loaded up into the bus to bring us to the bar, he arrived with a group of five other guys. He claimed that they happened to be on vacation in Tulum as well. I call bullshit on that, but it's not my coin nor Arnold's he's spending so I'm letting it slide, but I'm keeping a watchful eye.

Arnold sits on the couch across from me, rubbing his hand back and forth across his low cut caesar with a dazed expression. We're here with close to twenty of his friends, colleagues, and clients. Everyone has been trying to celebrate him, but his demeanor has left them with no option but to give him a wide berth.

Cortez and his boys walk over to the couches and Cortez holds out a rum and coke for Arnold.

"Here you go, cuz. I got you a re-up."

"Yo, he's had enough," I state, no room for argument in my tone.

Cortez scrutinizes me from head to toe. "You his daddy or something? You don't look like my uncle Marquise, but I don't know. Maybe y'all switched bodies or some shit."

His boys co-sign his dumbass with a collective cackle.

"He's damn near incoherent. He needs to sober up."

"Says who?"

I lean forward, folding my arms between my legs. "Says me."

He puffs his chest out in a show of strength, but I clock the gulp of air he swallows. His friends constrict their eyes at me looking between us, waiting for their boy to put me in my place. Little do they know their fearless leader is nothing more than a punk ass bitch.

Jalen, Christian, Micah, Troy, and one of Arnold's clients, pro football player, Nick Graves, flag me on the couch. They don't say anything, but their presence is enough to let Cortez's boys know they'd be foolish to make a move.

Cortez coughs into his elbow. "Whatever, man. This is supposed to be a bachelor party. We're here to turn the fuck up. Y'all like to be lame as fuck, I see."

Arnold groans, reminding everyone that he was the original reason behind this tension. "I'm good, y'all." His eyes close as he says something else that no one can hear or understand.

Cortez grins, sliding down into the seat next to Arnold. "See? He's good." I send a death glare his way, prompting him to lift his hands in surrender. "Anyway, yo Arnold, your girl keeps some bad bitches in her circle, huh?"

The rest of the clown squad let out whistles and howls of agreement, confirming my suspicions that they've been around for a while, because how else would they have seen the women Amerie hangs around? A growl hums beside me and I turn to see Micah watching them with barely veiled fury.

"Uh, sure, yeah," Arnold agrees.

Cortez strokes the lines of his goatee with a move straight out of a bad kung fu movie. "They all bad as fuck. That one bitch, what's her name? Dani? I'd bend her Amazonian ass over any day."

"Watch your mouth," Micah warns.

"Oh shit, son. That's you?" He jokes, the laughter of his goons boosting his confidence.

"No. But you need to watch how you talk about women when you're around me. I don't play that shit." We all echo his comment.

He pretends to shiver in fear, cackling at his own antics. "Right, right. My bad. What about Miss Evelyn? Any of you got eyes on her? She fine as hell but she kinda mouthy. Those the ones that look the best with my dick in their mouth."

"You must not value your life, huh?" Jalen asks, his voice a deathly low rumble.

"Yo, Arnold, is this who you spend your time with? Who the fuck is this clown?" Nick asks.

"Watch who you calling a clown, fool." This man is a fucking idiot. Nick Graves is lethal; he's one of the biggest linemen in the game and he's got about six inches and one hundred and fifty pounds on Cortez. He really doesn't value his life.

Arnold runs his hands along his head again. "He's my cousin. He's just d-drunk." No, he's an asshole. That's his default, it's just dialed up because he's drunk.

"Shit, I'm drunk and I'm not saying dumb shit like this," Troy adds.

"Facts," Christian agrees.

Jalen's eyes remain locked in on Cortez. "I'm waiting on your answer. Do you value your life or nah?"

Cortez's eyes wander around the room, careful not to land on Jalen. I grip my glass tighter in my hand, wishing it were Cortez's skull.

"Y'all too sensitive for me. I'm just speaking my mind, I ain't know that was against the law. Shit. I'm not checking for neither of them anyway." He rubs his hands together in front of his chest. "Nah, I'm really checking for Janelle's fine ass. She thick as a bitch."

I crack the knuckles on my free hand because I know before the end of the night they'll be introduced to Cortez's face. I gulp down the rest of my drink, sniffing as I sit the glass on the table in front of me.

One of the goons claps hands with Cortez at that statement, earning a growl from me.

"That bout to be you, my boy?" Another one of the goons asks.

"Hell yeah, by the time this wedding is over, I'ma have fucked her seven different ways. Arnold, my boy, tell me, how was the pussy? Was that shit tight or was it whack? Is that why you left ol' girl for her sister? I hate when bad bitches have weak ass pussy."

Arnold's head snaps up at that.

"Cortez."

Everyone's eyes turn to me. Christian, Troy, and Nick look concerned. The goons look amused. Jalen and Micah are the only ones who know how close to death Cortez is right now.

"Think carefully about the next words you say. You've already been warned once about watching your mouth. If I have to tell you, I'ma speak in a language I know you understand." Cortez has gotten his ass beat for his mouth before but if I do it, I'll make sure the lesson sticks.

One of the goons laughs but quickly cuts it off when the other ones don't join.

"You threatening me over some pussy?"

I sit on the edge of my seat. "I don't make threats."

He runs his tongue over his teeth, contemplating his next move. "I don't see what the problem is. Arnold got to tap both Cross sisters. I'm just saying if we passing pussy around…"

No one hears the end of Cortez's sentence because my fist ramming into his face cuts it off. I hear protests from both sides of me. Glass shatters around me and I hear bodies hitting the ground, signifying my boys are probably fighting Cortez's to keep them away from the two of us. Nothing could get me off Cortez's ass right now.

He tries to grab my shirt to give himself some leverage, but I knock his hand down. I allow my rage to take over until I'm literally blinded by it. All

I see is red. I do hear him though. I hear his whimpers of pain and the sound of his bones cracking beneath the weight of my fist. They mingle like an orchestra in my ears, until I feel fingers pressing into my back and shoulders, trying to pull me back.

"Rome, Rome! Let him go! He's out." I recognize Jalen's voice, briefly piercing the haze around me. When I look down at Cortez's face, I see a bloody mass. His eye is already swollen shut and I can't even tell where all the blood is pooling from.

I allow the guys to pull me up and away from Cortez's limp body. "We gotta go," Christian announces, eyes searching the bar for police.

I lose a chunk of time in the hysteria that ensues. I don't remember leaving the bar or ending up at the local police station. I don't remember speaking to anyone or anyone speaking to me.

What I do know is that she's here. Her energy latches onto mine, shifting it to something less dangerous and more recognizable. As I walk out of the cell block behind Troy and Christian, I scan the area until I spot her.

My mouth tips up into a grin at the sight of her dressed in a black bustier top, waist beads, severely ripped jeans, and heels. Those damn waist beads.

Amerie runs into Arnold's arms. He seems to have completely sobered up now, so that's one less fight we'll have to deal with tonight. She stares at the bruise on his cheek, her eyes stormy as she runs her fingers over it.

"Are y'all okay?" Eve asks.

"Let's get out of here before we say anything," Jalen says.

We all pile into the party bus that the ladies were using for their night out. Apparently, the rest of Arnold's guests got out before the cops arrived. Jalen managed to get Nick out so he wouldn't end up on the news and jeopardize his season, so it's just me, Jalen, Micah, Christian, Arnold, and Troy. Janelle, Eve, Amerie, Dani, and Nova left their other friends at the bar. They plan to send the bus back for them once we get back to the hotel.

Janelle sits beside me on the bus, the only parts of our bodies touching are our knees but her support rolls over me in waves, coating me in its warmth.

Christian fills the ladies in on the events of the night. I don't bother to chime in, but I know he's exaggerating some of the details. When he shares the details of what Cortez said about the women, I can feel my fists beginning to itch with the need to hit him again, but Janelle lays her hand on my knee, soothing the ache.

"Rome beat the bricks off that man. I'm telling you he hulked the fuck out. There was a whole steel table separating him from Cortez and he moved that shit out of his way like it was a piece of paper."

"That's what ol' Baby Legs O'Houlihan gets," Eve huffs.

"Not Baby Legs O'Houlihan. Please," Dani snorts.

Eve does her best Roger from "American Dad" impression, leaving everyone in stitches.

"Thanks for coming through for us ladies," Micah says.

"We weren't gonna leave y'all in a cell all night. We didn't realize Jalen was gonna be able to pull strings to get you out though," Dani asserts.

"I mean, I would've gladly left Christian in a cell for the rest of eternity, but I was told that wasn't an option," Eve shrugs.

"No man left behind, sweetheart," he taunts.

"Pretty sure you were left behind in school but small wins, I guess."

The two of them fall into their usual banter while the rest of the bus remains quiet, eerily quiet. Dani, Troy, and Micah seem to be at peace, but there's a tension floating between Amerie, Arnold, and Janelle. Janelle won't even look at the two of them, despite the fact that Amerie is burning a hole on the side of her face with her stare.

We get back to the hotel and everyone rushes off the bus. "Hey, Troy," I call. He stops and moves to stand in front of me by the side of the bus. "'Preciate you having our back. You didn't have to do that."

"It was nothing. Guys like that make me fucking sick so I was happy to help. I would've done the same thing if I were you."

"If you were me?"

He pins me with a knowing stare. "I think you know what I mean."

I consider his words, choosing to acknowledge them with only a laugh. "Good lookin out," I offer him my hand and he takes it, pulling me into an embrace.

When I step into the bright entrance of the lobby, Janelle steps around the corner holding a blue box. She smiles as she inclines her head for me to follow her.

Amerie, hand in hand with Arnold, marches over to Janelle with a desperate smile. "Janelle, can we talk?"

"No."

Amerie's jaw hits the ground as she watches Janelle's back disappear around the corner. I step around her, not caring if she sees me trying to catch up with Janelle. Right now, we need each other and that's the only thing that matters.

She leaves her door open for me as she steps inside, stripping off her rings and earrings but leaving her waist beads on.

I close the door behind me and she grabs my hands, inspecting my busted knuckles. "Come on, Caveman."

I follow her to her large bathroom where she instructs me to sit on the closed toilet seat. She fills the basin of the sink up with cold water and lays a hand towel inside of it, wringing it dry, and then filling it with ice. Then, she opens the blue box she had with her, revealing it to be a first aid kit.

"J, you don't have to do that. I'm okay."

"Shhh. I don't wanna hear it."

"You don't?"

"Let me pour into you the way you do for me."

She holds the makeshift ice pack to my knuckles, using her free hand to massage my forearm.

"Where'd you get the first aid kit?"

"Javier. The man has everything on hand. How's that feel?" She gestures toward my hand with her head.

"Stings a little but it's fine. Nothing I can't handle."

"That's right. Maybe I should call you Hulk instead of Caveman."

I chuckle. "You can call me whatever you want, J."

She lifts the ice from my knuckles, tossing it back into the sink and then she grabs some cream and bandages from the first aid kit, gingerly patching me up. "Mhmm, remember you said that." She bends down to press a soft kiss against my now bandaged hand and then another one on my lips. "Thank you. You having my back like that when I wasn't even around means more to me than you will ever know."

"You never have to thank me for that. You just have to trust me to keep doing it."

A tear slips down the side of her cheek, so I lift my good hand to stop it and she leans into it. The trance doesn't last long because she sucks in a deep breath, inspecting her handiwork before grasping my uninjured hand and pulling me into the bedroom. She pushes me down on the bed and crawls behind me, lifting the hem of my shirt.

"You trying to take advantage of me? Because I'll allow it," I joke.

"Well," A slightly warm liquid hits my back as Janelle's voice tickles my eardrum. "Some kind, considerate, and caring man had some massage oils sent to me earlier so now I'm going to use them to help you relax."

"Really? That sounds like a guy you should take a chance on."

"You think so? See, I was kinda torn between him and the guy who puts men in the hospital for talking bad about me. I don't know, this could be the beginning of my dark romance era."

"Ohh, I get it. I think you're confused. You're thinking those are two different guys."

She applies a pressure that makes me putty in her hands. I groan with every knot that comes loose under her touch. "They're not?"

"Nah. They're clearly the same guy. They have the same motivation and everything."

"And what's that?"

"You."

She meets my eyes in the full-length mirror facing us, smiling shyly. "That's something to consider."

"I hope so." Her hands continue working their magic on me. I start to change the subject several times but keep losing my train of thought the deeper she kneads my skin. "Damn, you're good at this."

She hums her agreement.

I use my good hand to reach up and cover her hand on my shoulder, stopping her motion. I can't think straight with her voodoo hands on me. "You wanna tell me what that was about with Amerie earlier?" The pride I felt at seeing her tell Amerie no without any further explanation was next level. I know it's probably shaking her at her core to be on the outs with her sister, but she did it anyway and stood firm on it.

She doesn't pull away from me even though her eyes appear somber. She meets my gaze head on and speaks her mind. "Yes, but I don't wanna waste any more energy on it right now," she takes a brief pause. "But I do need to tell you something about Arnold."

A shrill tone fills the room and we both glance over at our ringing phones. My call is coming from Christian whereas hers is coming from Dani, but they have the same message. Arnold has called a family meeting.

The hotel has a large outdoor seating area, partially covered by a bamboo ceiling and filled with velvet lined loveseats and wooden benches. The area is closed off at night, but I guess Arnold found a way to grant us access because that's where this family meeting is being held. Janelle and I arrive together, followed by Troy. Arnold and Amerie are standing beneath a few of the light fixtures, looking like they're about to tell us which one of us has been voted off the island.

Eve, Dani, Micah, Christian, Troy, Nova, the Cross', Arnold's parents, and his aunt and uncle all watch with rapt attention.

"Sorry to call you all here but we figured it'd be easier just to tell everyone at once instead of trying to tell you all individually."

"Well, first, Arnold wants to say something to you all directly," Amerie comments.

"Yes, um, I just wanna say I'm sorry for my actions tonight and for my cousin's actions." His comment is a blanket statement to everyone; however, Janelle scoffs quietly. "Now, moving on to our announcement. Cortez is in the hospital." He pauses and I'm not sure why because everyone knows he's in the hospital and no one cares. His own parents don't even seem concerned.

His mom chimes in at that moment. "Yes, and he won't be making any statements to the police so anyone who might've been worried about that can rest assured." She regards everyone as she speaks but her stare lingers on me. It's a sweet gesture, but unnecessary. I wouldn't have cared even if he had made a statement. I'm not afraid of the Cortez's of the world. Her husband drapes his arm over her shoulder and turns her to face Arnold again.

"Okay. Is that all?" Nova asks.

"I also wanted to let everyone know that I told Cortez he's not welcome to the wedding. He'll probably be transferring to a hospital back home anyway, but I just wanted to share that. I hired security to make sure his friends don't show up at the hotel or the wedding either. If you see them, though, please let me know."

Everyone murmurs their agreement, not really moved by this announcement. Amerie thanks us for coming down and dismisses us. As Janelle's parents move to leave, her dad spots her and runs over to offer her a comforting hug. Her mom doesn't approach but she watches Janelle with a wistful smile, her eyes shine with unshed tears. Janelle and I haven't had a chance to talk about the details of her discussion with her mom, but I can tell her mom doesn't know how to proceed from here. It seems to me that Amerie learned her way of dropping tears to get her way from their mom.

Marquise makes a beeline for me, offering me his fist and he laughs when I hold out my bandaged hand to him.

He leans in close, whispering, "Long time coming if you ask me," before sending a nod Janelle's way and walking back to the hotel.

Everyone else clears out relatively fast but Janelle and I stay put.

"It's been a long day," she says.

"It has. How do you wanna end it?" She was trying to tell me something before this little press conference, but her eyes are so hooded with fatigue, I know she's drained. Frankly, the exhaustion is starting to set in on my own shoulders, too.

She takes a step so that she and I are toe to toe. I wrap my arms around her waist, leaning my hands on her ass, and she locks her arms behind my neck.

"With you."

"That was a given."

She snorts. "I ain't gon hold you, I'm so tired the room feels like it's miles away. I'm about to sleep on one of those couches for the night. They look comfy." She motions her head toward the velvet loveseats.

I shake my head at her dramatics. "If you wanted a ride, you could've just said that."

I settle my arms under her ass to lift her up, but she wiggles in my hold. "No, dummy, your hand!"

"Fuck the hand. Come here." I lift her up my body until her legs wrap around my waist. Our lips connect in a hungry kiss, our tongues fighting for purchase. I didn't even realize I was moving us backward until I stumble into one of the couches. The momentum lands me straight on my back so I brace my hands on her to make sure the fall doesn't jostle her too much.

She laughs into my mouth. "Weren't you supposed to be giving me a ride back to the room?"

"Well, you did say the couches looked comfortable. I was just testing that theory."

"Mmm, yeah, I was right. It'd be a shame to waste a perfectly good couch."

"A damn shame." She sucks my lower lip into the wet heat of her mouth, moaning around it.

"What the fuck?!"

Our eyes pop open at the sound of a shriek that's about to make our long night even longer.

CHAPTER THIRTEEN

Janelle

"**W**HAT THE FUCK IS GOING ON?!" AMERIE SHRIEKS AGAIN, HER voice crashing down around me like a bucket of ice water.

I take my time dismounting from Rome's lap because I know the minute I acknowledge Ri's presence, the delicate tatters of our relationship will disintegrate into dust. I thought I would be despondent if Rome and I ever got caught because I thought it would drive a wedge between me, my sister, and my mom. Now, severing ties with them brings me an odd feeling of peace. I never thought I'd tell my own sister I'm not coming to her wedding, but I haven't questioned that decision since I said it.

Rome lets out a tortured groan and it only takes me a moment to realize why. Not only is Ri standing there but so are Arnold, Evie, Dani, Micah, Christian, and Jalen. Of course.

"I tried to stop her," Evie grimaces.

Ri rounds on her, steam practically rolling out of her ears. If she were a little lighter, her face would probably be bright red right now.

"You knew about this?!" My teeth rattle from the sheer volume of her voice.

"Ri, please," Dani begs. "You're loud as hell. Let's just dial it down a few."

"Did you know about this too? Did all my friends know about this?"

"Maybe if you weren't such an asshole to her, she would've told her sister instead of me," Evie jeers.

"I didn't know but I'm not bothered by it either. Who cares?"

"I care!" Her voice goes up another octave. A blood vessel is about to pop in her forehead and glass is about to start shattering at these volumes. Christian winces from the sound, taking a step away from her. Jalen and Micah start looking back the way I assume they came, plotting their exit.

Rome rubs soft circles on my lower back. I want him closer to me, so I lean back to connect my back with his chest. I know my bold behavior shocks him, but we've already been exposed. What other fucks do I have to give?

"And then they just sit there all cuddled up, not even trying to explain themselves," Ri chastises.

"Why would we explain ourselves? We're grown ass adults," Rome asks, his voice calm and unaffected, which only enrages Ri more.

"Grown ass adults but you're sneaking around like children. How long has this been going on?"

Neither of us answers her. We don't owe her that. We don't owe her anything.

She scoffs at our lack of response. "You know what, Janelle? You're a fucking con-artist."

"The fuck?" Rome grasps my arm to keep me from jumping up from my seat. How did I become a con-artist for not telling her who I'm sleeping with?

"Jesus, okay, Ri. Enough," Dani whines.

"Yeah, it's truly not that deep," Evie presses.

"No, let her speak her piece. Say what you have to say, Amerie," I demand.

She points her pointer finger in my direction, spit flying out of her mouth as she yells. "You heard me the first time. You're a con artist! You really had me feeling bad for you and questioning my relationship when you told me Arnold tried to kiss you but you're the one who's a liar."

"What?" Rome's voice is like a bolt of lightning, striking the epicenter and destroying everything in its path. Now it's my turn to keep him from getting up from his seat. He fights my hold, but I turn to face him, begging him with my eyes to stay with me.

Chaos erupts all around us. Everyone starts talking at once.

"That's foul, bruh," Micah shakes his head.

"What the hell is wrong with you?" Dani shouts.

"Shut up," Ri whispers. No one seems to hear her except me.

"Yo, Rome, what you wanna do?" Jalen asks. I keep a firm grasp on Rome, watching his shaky breaths return to an even tempo before he offers Jalen a slight shake of his head and I turn back to face everyone.

"Shut up," Ri says again. Her voice is a little louder this time but still, no one hears her.

"Mhm, I would expect this from your dirty dick friend, but you, Arnold?" Evie says, looking between Arnold and Christian with disgust.

"My dick's clean," Christian rebuts. "But yeah, bruh, I wouldn't even do that shit," he says to Arnold.

"Yes the fuck you would," Evie argues.

"Shut up!" Ri screams at the top of her lungs. Everyone's eyes cut over to her. Evie plants her hands on her hips, daring Ri to say something else she doesn't like. "Everyone shut up. You're all just feeding into Janelle's lies."

Arnold tips his head to the ceiling, seeking strength from a higher power, I guess.

"So I'm a liar, Arnold? Is that what we're doing now?"

He rubs his hand down his face. "Fuck," he drags out the word.

The rise and fall of Rome's chest becomes so erratic, I know I'm losing my hold on him. He's clenching his fist so tight I can hear the bandage stretching beyond its capacity.

"He touched you." He says, his voice low and gravelly in my ear. It's not a question. Unlike my own sister, Rome wouldn't question me on something like this. He knows I'm telling the truth and he's trying to figure out how he's going to handle it.

"He tried to kiss me. I slapped him and got him out of my room." A deep snarl escapes his throat.

"Ugh!" Ri lets out a banshee cry, having heard my response to Rome. "Stop saying that, it's not true."

She's determined to be delusional and I'm not interested in being the one to coax her back down to reality. If she's happy in her fantasy land, so be it.

"You got it, Ri. I'll stop. Are we done here?"

Everyone's voices keep buzzing around in my head, whispering their two cents and protests. I rub firm circles into my temples, trying to keep the impending headache at bay.

She huffs. "I'm so done with you. I can't believe you betrayed my trust for a fling."

"Betrayed **your** trust?" My hands fall to my sides. "That's it. Everyone out. Everyone get out now." She can spin the story however she wants to everyone later. When I leave this seat, I will have freed myself from her for good.

"You gonna be okay?" Rome asks. I take a moment to study him. I can feel his chest buzzing with ire. His eyes are drilling into the depths of Arnold's soul and yet instead of jumping at the chance to confront him like I know he wants to, he waits to see if I need him more. I keep telling myself these past two weeks have been too good to be true. I'm so used to being slowly drained dry that the feeling of someone breathing life into me is a foreign concept.

Leaning my forehead against his, I close my eyes and breathe him in. "I'm gonna be just fine. Are you?"

"Depends on what he has to say."

"You've hit your quota on the number of guys you can send to the hospital, okay? I was joking about the dark romance thing."

He laughs as he stands from the couch, keeping his gaze on me as he moves toward our lingering friends. "That's to be discussed at the next book club, J."

"The book club of just you and I?"

"Who else do we need?"

"Damn, how did I miss them being all lovey dovey like that?" Christian questions.

Evie shoves him in the chest. "Get your nosey ass outta here." She continues pushing him until they're out of sight.

A lifetime seems to pass before Ri and I so much as blink. Neither one of us wants to concede power to the other, but since I no longer feel the need to control the outcome, I decide to break the silence.

The moment I open my mouth; however, it's Ri's words that come out first. "Why do you have to have everything?"

She's a lot less brazen now. Her shoulders are slumped forward in defeat. Her downcast eyes are void of any fight.

"What is that supposed to mean?"

"You couldn't just let me have one thing. You had to prove to everyone that not only could you have my soon-to-be husband if you wanted, but you could have his best friend as well. Who's next? Micah? Christian? Hell, why don't you go for Arnold's dad? That'll really show him."

I take a moment to will my fists back to my lap when they really want to aim right at Ri's jaw. "You know, Ri, a day ago a comment like that from you would've sliced me to my core. But now, I realize that your opinion of me doesn't define me. I keep trying to save a relationship that should've died a long time ago. I'm done with that."

"It's just that easy for you to cut me off?"

"It's not easy at all. But at this point it's either lose you or lose me. And whether you and Mom believe I deserve it or not, I love me. A whole lot. I'm not willing to come in second anymore."

She sucks in a breath, nodding slowly. "I wish I could do that. I wish I could cut people off and know that I'm gonna be better for it, but I'm not like you."

"Why do you think that? Why do you and Mom think that I'm some unfeeling robot?"

"Because everything just comes so easily to you. You wanted to go to medical school? You got into your first choice and then your field of choice like that," she snaps her fingers.

It's so funny to me that just because they weren't there for my struggles, they think they don't exist. I've overcome a lot in my life. I've survived not feeling enough in my mom's eyes. I've cried over plenty of boys. I've shed literal blood, sweat, and tears during my med school journey. I've suffered heartaches and growing pains. I've needed my mom and sister to be a support system more times than I can count. The problem lies within the fact that I never felt they could fulfill that need. I never felt important enough to them to ask.

"I worked my ass off to get where I am in my career, it didn't come easily. And why are you talking about my career like you don't own a whole business?"

She lets out a stony-faced laugh. "Yeah, and it's failing."

"What?"

"The line is not doing as well as I'd hoped. It's already been taken out of a few department stores and business is dry. Hell, the only reason I'm still afloat right now is because Arnold pays all the bills."

"Ri, why didn't you tell me this?"

"Why do you think none of my investors, clients, or friends in the industry were invited to the wedding? It's because they either don't exist anymore, or I didn't want to risk them exposing me to you or Mom."

"I could've helped though."

"I didn't want your help. It's embarrassing to always have to rely on my little sister for help. I'm the big sister. You're supposed to come to me. But I guess I never inspired that in you."

My mind is blown. I never knew her line was struggling so badly. She put her heart and soul into launching it, so I know it's eating her up not to see the results she wanted.

I hate that this is where we've ended up. This place where I want to offer my sister comfort but don't feel safe doing so. She's standing inches away from me, but we are miles apart.

"Okay, fine. You didn't want my help. But what about anyone else's? Did you tell Mom and Dad? Did you tell Dani and Evie? Dani has a platform with millions of followers, she could've easily put you on. And Evie is a beast with marketing and graphic design. She could've helped with a rebrand."

She hangs her head in shame. "No. It was bad enough having to tell Arnold that he had to cover all of our expenses because I couldn't contribute. You think I wanted to admit failure to our friends? Our very successful friends? And no, I didn't tell Mom and Dad. I was trying to be more like you and handle it myself."

Now things are starting to make more sense. She's been under an incredible amount of stress not only trying to keep her business afloat but also trying to hide her struggles from everyone around her. I know how exhausting that is, and I do sympathize with her, but I never took my frustrations out on her. I can't keep giving her passes for how she's treated me.

"Anything would've been better than how you went about it."

"I know, I know. I've been awful to Arnold, too. I think it's because I couldn't contribute financially to our lives together. I felt the need to be in control of something. I needed to have a handle on something, so I tried to control every aspect of his life, including talking to you. I was so terrified he would come to his senses and leave me that I damn near made it happen." She twists her face up into a frown. "I know he tried to kiss you. I believed you the minute you said it, but I didn't want to see my greatest fear coming true."

"Wow," I huff. "You and Mom went to the same school of gaslighting." What am I saying? Mom probably taught the class.

"Pretty much. He and I talked before we called that damn meeting about Cortez and he told me everything."

"And?"

"He claims he doesn't love you. He was just trying to sabotage our relationship because I scared him."

I can believe that. I never believed what he said for a second. I just couldn't believe he had the balls to try to use me to run from my sister.

"I don't know what I'm supposed to say to all of this, Ri."

"Me either. I just got tired of holding it all in."

"I know the feeling."

She flops down on the couch beside me with a sharp exhale. "I'm sorry." I stare at her, unflinching. Her words circle around me, seeking a soft place to land but find nothing but hard ridges. "I just figured if this is the end of you and me then you should know how sorry I am. For everything. I never meant to fall in love with Arnold. I hated myself for falling for the one guy I shouldn't have, and I just kept expecting you to hate me for it too, so I wanted to hate you first. I wasted so much time and I'm sorry."

I'm not sure what she expects from me after this declaration. I can't tell her it's okay because it's not. I can't tell her I forgive her because I don't, at least not yet. All of this animosity could've been avoided if she had just talked to me.

Sitting here looking at this woman who I love with my whole heart, I see a glimpse of the girl I used to call my best friend. I hope she finds her way back to that girl one day, but I can't be present while she searches for her.

"Goodbye, Ri."

CHAPTER FOURTEEN

Rome

THE MOMENT WE STEP INTO THE HOTEL, I STUFF MY HANDS IN MY pockets. My gaze is fixated on Arnold as I take measured steps toward him. His eyes widen at my approach and he takes calculated steps backward, his hands lifted in front of him.

"Rome, look. I'm sorry, okay? I didn't know about you and Janelle."

"So that gives you a right to touch her?"

"No. I know I fucked up. You don't have to tell me."

Rage constricts all the air in my lungs as I picture Arnold cornering Janelle. I picture him invading her space so aggressively that she had to slap him to break free. My steps become heavy as the image of him allowing his fiancé to disparage her own sister in front of us like he was an innocent bystander plays on a loop in my mind.

"Then why did you do it? Coming between sisters is fucked up, Arnold," Christian reprimands. Arnold backs himself against a wall, the rest of us forming a semi-circle around him.

"Coming between sisters again, you mean," Jalen adds.

"I know, I know," he laments.

"Then why?"

"I wanted her to tell Ri!" He shouts, slamming his fist into his palm and shaking his head. "I wanted her to tell Ri so that Ri would break off the engagement and I wouldn't have to."

In the blink of an eye, I have the front of Arnold's shirt balled up in my fist, his feet an inch off the ground. The guys grab my arms, trying to separate us, but I make no moves to hit him. I just want him to hear me.

"Janelle is not yours."

"I know."

"She is not a toy that you can use as a pawn in your fucked up relationship."

"I know."

"If you want to end your engagement, be a man and do it yourself."

"That's the thing," he coughs from the pressure I have against his neck. I loosen it enough to let him breathe, but not enough that he can break free. "I don't wanna end my engagement. I love Amerie, I really do. I just panicked, okay? Things have been so fucked up lately with the stuff she has going on, and it was just a lot to deal with. I don't want out."

I tilt my head, not recognizing the man in front of me. This wedding has brought out the worst in both of them. "I don't really give a fuck what you two have going on. Janelle is a human being. That's a fact that you, Amerie, and their damn mother seem to keep forgetting, and if I have to remove you all from her life myself to give her some semblance of peace, I will."

"That would kill Ri." I harden my glare at him. "I get it, I do. I'm sorry."

"That sorry don't mean shit to me. Save that for Janelle and your wife." I release him from my grip, and he wobbles slightly on his ankle.

Arnold and I will be fine. Despite the way he's acted on this trip, I know my friend. He wants to appear perfect to the world, but he's not. He's just a man who makes mistakes and eventually he gets them right. The only thing he needs do to make it right with me is make it right with Janelle. I brush my hands down the front of my shirt and head in the direction of my room.

"This is going in my toast, too!" Jalen yells after me. I smile, throwing up a middle finger as I go.

A little while later, Janelle finally shows up at her door. Her face looks devoid of any emotions until she sees me sitting in front of her door and I'm rewarded with a colorful smile.

"You waited up for me?"

"Of course."

"And you brought your stuff?" She says, looking at my suitcase stacked by her door.

"I figured we could stop pretending we're spending the night apart now."

She kisses me deeply, pulling away with my bottom lip between her teeth. "You figured right."

She leads me inside where we change into our bathing suits and wade into her pool. With the cool touch of marble at our backs and warm water at our hips, she unburdens herself. She tells me about her fallout with her mom, her fallout with Amerie, and her decision not to attend the wedding. When her voice starts to crack, I pull her into me, giving her all my strength as she allows her body to be racked with sobs.

"I know it hurts right now, but I am so fucking proud of you."

She lifts her head from my shoulder, the hint of smile on her lips.

"Thank you. I'm proud of me too."

I kiss the tip of her nose, wiping her tears away with my hands. She sniffles, a giggle taking over her face. "You are…unexpected, Rome."

I feel the same way about her. I think a part of me knew when I met her that we would end up here and that's why I stayed away. This wedding may be a complete shit show but I'm thankful that it brought me here, to her. "In a good way?"

"In the best way."

She pulls my lips down to hers, claiming my mouth in a fiery kiss. Her lips immediately open for me when I press my tongue along the seam.

She moans around my tongue, hiking her leg up my side so that I can feel the heat of her pussy.

Without breaking our kiss, she glides her hand under the waistband of my shorts, taking my length in her hands.

Her fingers flex and tighten over my dick, squeezing and tugging with a firmness that makes my head fall backward.

Her lips fall to my jawline, leaving a trail of kisses across it and my neck. Forcing myself out of the trance she put me in, I lift her up onto the edge of the pool, ripping her bottoms down her legs and pulling the cups of her bikini top down.

We moan together when I bend to take her hardened nipple in my mouth at the same time that she lines me up at her entrance and surges her hips up. I wrap my arms around her waist and pull her down into the water, switching our positions so that my back is against the wall.

The water comes up to my neck while her breasts dip in and out of the water with every bounce. I brace my hands on her hips, using the waves of the water to give her momentum.

She looks sexy as hell like this. The moonlight bathing her in its glow, the droplets of water on her skin glistening like diamonds, her cries of pleasure unrestrained. When her orgasm takes over, I can see the reflection of the stars in her eyes, letting me know I'm home.

The wedding is finally here. I never thought I'd say this but I'm ready to get the fuck out of Tulum.

I glance over at Janelle, lying in bed pretending to be completely engulfed in her Kindle. Her braids are tied up in her bonnet and she's wearing nothing but one of my t-shirts.

She thinks I haven't noticed her peeking at me every few seconds as I get ready to go meet the guys. I glance down at my watch, noting that the woman should be meeting in the bridal suite in just thirty minutes. If she wanted to change her mind there's plenty of time to do so, but I won't mention that to her. She doesn't need me to make her question herself. Whether or not she chooses to come, I stand by her decision one hundred percent.

Kneeling on the bed by her side, I hover over her until she leans up to look at me. "I'll see you later. Want me to bring you a plate? I'll walk right out with it."

She chuckles. "I think I can venture into town if I get hungry. Thank you anyway."

"Okayyyy, if you say so."

"But if you wanted to bring me a slice of cake, I wouldn't be mad at it."

"Got you," I say, giving her a quick kiss and going back for two more before leaving her to her book.

Arnold looks ten times better today than he has the whole trip. He seems lighter on his feet and his smile comes a lot easier. He claims that he and Amerie had a heart-to-heart last night and laid everything on the line. The day before your wedding is cutting it close to me but I'm glad they finally figured their shit out.

The hotel will serve as the backdrop for today's festivities. The ceremony will take place on the beach while the reception will take place in the restaurant which has been closed to the public for the occasion.

The barber Arnold hired for the ceremony comes to the groom's parlor to clean up all of our cuts and beards. Marquise stops by to give us all cigars, which we enjoy before suiting up.

"Arnold, I don't mean to show you up on your own wedding day, but I am killing this suit, my boy," Christian says, observing himself in the full-length mirror. Our suits are a hunter green color with mock neck collars and orange boutonnieres.

"Stupid ass," Micah mocks.

"Yeah, yeah, you can have all the attention today. There's only one person I'm checking for," Arnold waves him off.

The head of the security team that Arnold hired for the ceremony pops up to tell Arnold the team completed another perimeter check so we're good to take our places on the beach.

"Hey, Rome, hold up a second," Arnold calls after me.

He waits until Micah and Christian leave the room to speak. "I just wanted to say thanks. I needed to get my head out of my ass, and you helped with that."

"Always happy to let you know when you're being an idiot, my guy."

He chortles at that, adjusting his sleeves on both sides. "I bet. How's

Janelle doing? I haven't had a chance to apologize to her yet, and I wasn't sure if stopping by her room was a good move."

"Probably not. She's good, though. As good as she can be considering."

He nods. "Do you think she and Ri will ever make up?"

"That's not for either of us to try to predict. They have to figure it out on their own and all parties need to accept the outcome, whatever it may be."

He studies me closely, his eyes squinting in concentration. "You really care about her, don't you?"

"I do," I offer.

He steps beside me, patting me on the back to guide me out. "I couldn't think of a better man for her."

The beach area has been transformed into a beautiful stage. A giant dark wood makeshift floor has been set up with rows of oak benches facing the platform where the ceremony will take place. A path branches off leading to the restaurants so that guests won't have to walk in the sand to get to the reception.

Behind the stage is a row of palm trees and at the edge of it is an archway covered in ivy along with white, brown, tan, and pale pink flowers.

I take my place beside Arnold and wait for the ceremony to start. The music begins and Evie is the first one down the aisle, waving to a few people as she does. Dani is next, owning the aisle like she's back on the runway.

I expect the music to change for Amerie's entrance, but it keeps going and Janelle steps onto the platform. She looks absolutely stunning. The sun is hitting her at just the right angle, making the bright orange of the wrap dress she's wearing accentuate her brown skin. Her braids fall against her bare shoulders in a half up, half down style that highlights the column of her neck and the deep slit of her dress demands attention as her thigh keeps playing peek-a-boo with me.

Her eyes never leave mine as she walks down the aisle, sending me a small wave that I return with a brilliant smile.

The song changes to "For You" by Kenny Lattimore and I'm sure Amerie looks beautiful in her wedding dress. I hear Arnold suck back a few tears so I offer him a comforting hand on the shoulder, but my focus is squarely on Janelle. I mouth 'you look beautiful' to her and she tips her head slightly. I only look away once Amerie takes her place in front of Arnold.

"I now pronounce you husband and wife. You may kiss the bride," the officiant announces at the end of the ceremony. Arnold grabs the sides of Amerie's face and kisses her passionately, prompting a loud round of applause from the audience. They hold their joined hands up to everyone and then walk down the aisle to get ready for the reception.

Janelle and I link arms and walk down the aisle after them. "So, what changed your mind?" I whisper.

She takes a moment to consider her answer. "Honestly, I did it for me. I still have hope that Ri and I will find our way back to each other. And if we do, I don't want to look back and have regrets about not going to her wedding. She only gets one, we hope," she laughs.

Satisfaction rolls over me at the fact that she's here for herself more than anything. She's earned the right to make decisions that serve her and only her.

"Well then, I'm glad you're here. One of Arnold's aunts gets really handsy when she's drunk so now, I can have you fight her off for me."

"Aww, that's so romantic," she taunts.

I drop a kiss on her forehead and lead her to the reception area.

The reception has gone well so far. The food is delicious and everyone is having a great time. Janelle's mom kept her distance; I have a feeling at the urge of her husband and Amerie has been busy mingling. She and Janelle did exchange a hug; however, when she came to our table.

After dinner, it's time for the toasts and Janelle opts to go first. The emcee introduces her and she takes the mic, standing by the DJ stand.

"Hi everyone, thank you for being here. My sister is a complicated woman. She's both loud and quiet. She's sweet but she's not to be messed with. She's got a soft center hidden beneath a few hard ridges. She also likes donut holes but not donuts, so she's a little weird as well." The crowd laughs at that. Amerie laughs as she dabs the corners of her eyes. "She's complicated but one thing that's not complicated about her is her love for Arnold. She loves him fiercely. She asked me if they were moving too fast when they got engaged three months after they started dating but to me when your soul finds its tether, too fast isn't a phrase that exists. I knew whoever was lucky enough to marry her would need to be up for an adventure. They'd need to challenge her. They'd need to be patient with her while she finds herself. Because she is still finding herself. She's still growing and learning things about herself every day. And she needed someone who not only accepted that about her but wanted to help her through her journey. She deserved that.

I knew Arnold was the right man for her because he didn't want to change her or rush her journey or stop it altogether. He wanted to nurture her and protect her. Most of all, he wanted to grow with her, because he's still learning too. That's all I can ask for in the person I give my best friend to.

Love is not easy. It's waking up every day and choosing the person beside you. You two have seen each other at your best and your worst and you're still here, choosing each other. I hope you never lose sight of that. I hope you keep choosing each other for the rest of your lives."

She raises her glass, prompting everyone to look through their glossy eyes to do the same. "Cheers to Amerie and Arnold. May your 'for better or worse' be far better than worse."

Everyone joins her in cheers. Amerie, her cheeks stained with tears, blows Janelle a kiss and Arnold sends her a nod of respect.

She offers them both a sincere smile and then finds her way back to me, kissing me in front of everyone.

"Nah, that's bullshit. There were definitely some tears going during my toast," I insist.

"No, baby, those were leftover tears from my toast. But your toast was cute," she says, her tone mocking. "You at least didn't get booed off the stage so be thankful for that."

"Cute? My nephew is cute. Puppies are cute. My toast wasn't cute."

She nods sympathetically. "Oh, right, your toast was grown and sexy. I'm so sorry."

I lean over in laughter. "She gets a little round of applause and she thinks she's the shit."

"Thinks. Tuh. You say you don't wanna be called cute, but you keep saying cute things."

I take a forkful of cake and shove it into her mouth. She cackles, some of the cake falling onto the table.

Arnold and Amerie left the reception an hour ago, allowing Janelle to come alive and fully enjoy herself. We've been dancing with our friends all night long, only taking breaks to refuel with more cake and alcohol.

I met the infamous Wheezie tonight via FaceTime as Janelle and Nova set up a video chat that would allow her to see the ceremony and the toasts. Wheezie wanted to know who the man was that her niece was tonguing down.

We haven't talked about it, but it seems like a given that Janelle and I will continue to see each other once we get back home. Everyone is treating us like we're already a couple and she doesn't seem to be running away from the idea.

I don't like to assume anything, though, so when Coco Jones' "ICU" starts to play, I hold out my hand and ask her to dance with me.

The look of bliss on her face as she sways in my arms lights a fire in my chest. "So, Janelle Cross, you've survived the wedding of the year. What's next for you?"

She tilts her head toward the ceiling, a smile playing on her lips. "Well, I'll probably go home and sleep for a full twenty-four hours."

"Fair."

"And then I'm gonna call about that building for Labor of Love."

"Good. I can't wait to see how that goes."

"Mhm. And I was kinda hoping that I would see more of this one guy but I don't know he's a very busy man," she shrugs.

The visions I have of a future with this woman take flight at that. I don't know where we'll go from here. I don't know what dating will look for us back in the real world, but I'm excited to find out.

"He'd be a fool to be too busy for you."

"Eh, we'll see, I guess. What about you? What's next for you, Rome?"

"I was thinking that when we get home you'd let me take you on a real date."

Her teeth sink into her bottom lip. "Is that right? Remind me again, am I still supposed to be giving you all my yes's?"

I grip her hips tighter and pull her in closer. "You're supposed to be giving me whatever answer feels right to you."

"Ahh okay. Well in that case," she pauses. "Yes."

EPILOGUE

Janelle
One year later

"S TOP, STOP, YOU'RE GONNA MESS UP MY OUTFIT," I WHINE BUT it turns into a whimper when Rome bites down on my shoulder blade.

"Mhm, I see no problem with that," he mumbles, his tongue flicking across the top of my breasts.

"Romeeee, I'm gonna be late!" I shout. Maybe being a little later won't be too bad. Being on time can't be better than the feeling of Rome's lips on me. *No. Get your ass moving.* I wiggle in his hold a bit more, groaning with displeasure.

He releases me with a groan, putting my blazer back in place. "Fine, I guess I'll be supportive of your dreams and shit and let you go," he teases.

I wipe the lipstick that I got on his lips off as I chuckle. "Your kindness will be rewarded later, I promise."

He kisses me again, getting more of my lipstick on him. "You got this."

"I love you," I say.

"I love you, too."

How surreal is it that I freely exchange I love you's with this man? The first time we said it was so unceremonious. He'd said it while walking me to my car after I'd spent the night at his place, as if we had been saying it for years. When I looked at him like he'd lost it, he just said he was tired of not speaking what was in his heart. He leapt. Because that's what he does. Rome is a leaper and that used to terrify me. But after finding my parachute, I've discovered that I'm a leaper too.

He hands me a cup of coffee and I walk out to my car.

It's been a little over a year since that trip to Tulum and Rome and I have made the most of it.

When we came back to Baltimore, he delivered on that first date taking me to an A.R. Washington book signing at Bookmarked and Busy and he's delivered countless dates since then.

I thought that we would struggle to make time for each other with our busy careers, but it's truly been an easy adjustment. Rome sets his own schedule so he's able to make time. I've even been able to travel with him a few times for conferences and interviews. I still work long hours at the private practice, but I've learned to use my time off appropriately. Also, once I transition to the health center full time, I'll have even more time.

Labor of Love is official. I was shocked to learn that the building I wanted for it, Rome already owned, so after a hard-fought battle with him to actually let me pay for it we got to work on the necessary renovations. Today, I'm using my day off to have a meeting at the building with my new office manager, Tamara, and the board of doctors I personally chose to work with me. In one month, we'll be open for business.

Six months after we started dating, Rome and I moved in together. Evie has a key to our place, but she's taken to calling first because she said a girl can only see her best friend's ass but so many times before she's permanently traumatized.

When I get to the Labor of Love building, I see that I have a text from Amerie.

> Ri: Want to get lunch tomorrow?

Honestly, the hardest part about being with Rome is navigating our relationship with Amerie and Arnold.

Rome and Arnold are still best friends and they're back to spending a lot of time together. Rome is once again a regular attendee of Arnold's game nights. Amerie and I aren't there in our relationship, but she's trying.

We're taking baby steps in mending what was broken. I've gone with her to a few of her therapy sessions, which have been a big help, but I'm still not in a place where I can say I fully trust her. I could see us getting there one day, though.

My mom and I have settled into a new normal. We see each other on holidays and birthdays and that's about it. I know it pains my dad to have us be so distant with each other, but I've accepted that sometimes being selfish is a good thing. I love my mom but she's not good for me and I'm not willing to give her access to my life anymore; not after she refused to change her ways once we came home. I can't force her to change. I can only change the way I deal with her. Ri still wants a relationship with her, and I don't begrudge her that. All I ask is that if she wants to maintain a relationship with me that she respects my boundaries when it comes to Mom. So far, she's done that.

I text her back that I'm not sure about lunch just yet and then I pocket my phone and head inside.

Later, Rome and I cook dinner together and when we're done eating we get a FaceTime call from Jalen and Kam.

"Killa Kam! What's up, my guy?" Rome answers.

"Hi, Uncle Rome! Hi, Janelle!" He waves excitedly into the camera, and I return it tenfold.

"Hey Kam, how are you? Watch any new movies lately?"

"There's this new indie slasher movie I wanna see. You wanna watch it with me?"

"Of course. Let's take Pops with us," I say.

He pulls his fist down in a 'yes' motion.

Jalen takes the phone out of his hand. "I feel like this is a movie he shouldn't be watching," he questions.

"Probably not. But you know Pops is gonna show it to him one way or the other."

"Y'all are gonna pay for all the therapy he's gonna need."

"Umm, no I won't because you're a billionaire but I got you on the moral support."

He laughs and hands the phone back to Kam. "Say good night," I hear him say in the background.

"Good night! Oh wait! Uncle Rome, did you do it?!"

Rome's eyes widen and Kam's soon follow. "Uh, no. Not yet."

"Oops."

Jalen grabs the phone and I hear him say he's sorry before he hangs up. "Did you do what?"

He scratches the back of his neck. "I, um, I created a new game. He was just wondering if I showed it to you."

"Oh, you did? That's cool. I didn't realize you were working on a new game."

"Yeah. Actually, I want you to beta test it for me."

My eyes bulge out of my head. "Rome, you know I don't like scary games."

"She watches horror movies but hates scary games. Make it make sense."

"Horror movies I get to sit back and watch everyone survive or die. In games, I actually have to participate. No thank you! Would you choose to put yourself in the middle of a horror movie?"

He shrugs with a laugh. "It might be fun." I roll my eyes, making him laugh harder. "Okay, fine, no horror games for you. Lucky for you, this isn't a horror game. I tried my hand at something new. It's a dating sim."

"A dating sim? **You** made a dating sim?" I've gotten him fully invested into reading smut. We went to A.R. Washington's party for the release of the third book in her series and we **both** got signed copies. He's watched me play other dating sims games like *College Craze,* so I know he would never refuse to make one of his own. I just wouldn't expect this to be the type of game he'd take the time to design himself.

"Yes, so will you test it for me? I need the eyes of a smut reader."

"Don't count yourself out, Mr. Filth Pusher himself." Our new favorite thing is recreating the spicy scenes we read about. Some of them have been sexy as hell. Some of them, we've discovered, are physically impossible.

"You want me to test it now?"

"Yep. Come on."

He leads me to his home office and sets the PC up for me. When the game loads up, I see that he's titled it *Only For the Week*. I turn to him with a smug smile. "Cute."

I press start on the game and I'm taken to a character creation screen. I make the character look exactly like me, which is easier than it usually is in other games, and I name her Janelle as well.

You're supposed to be able to choose from a plethora of love interests in the game but the only option appears to be a character named Rome who looks exactly like Rome. I cut my eyes to him. "You better change that when you release the game. I'm not about to have thousands of women dating you."

He chuckles and kisses my forehead. "That's just for you. I didn't feel like uploading all the other character options just yet."

"Mhmm, I'm watching you."

I turn back to the screen and Rome disappears behind me.

I become engulfed in the game. It's so realistic. My character and Rome's character go on a lot of dates, some of them being exact replicas of dates he and I have taken in real life. Saying and doing things to build your characters' bond earns you points and those points lead to achievements. When I hit certain achievements, it provides cut scenes showing our characters moving to the next phase of our relationship. The cut scene for our characters moving in together showed them dancing in the living room, surrounded by her boxes, which is exactly what we did the night I moved into his place.

"Damn, this game is moving so fast. I kinda wanna slow it down a little bit. Or is the point to get people to play it through several times trying to get different achievements or different partners?"

He doesn't answer my question but I'm too enraptured to care.

I hit another achievement, prompting another cut scene. This one looks different than the others though. Instead of playing like a movie, it shows the Rome character getting on one knee in their house and then the title screen pops back up. Part of the title falls away, though, and changes so that it reads *Only Forever* instead.

A menu screen pops up that reads "Do you want to continue?" with yes or no options underneath.

I click yes but nothing happens. The Rome character just remains on bended knee with a smile on his face and a ring in his hand.

"Wait, what? Is it over? Why didn't it continue when I clicked yes?" I tap the screen a bunch of times, hoping to make something happen but it doesn't change.

"Because it hasn't happened yet." I hear him say behind me.

"What?"

I spin around to look at him but damn near fall over when I see him in the same position the Rome character was in the game. He's on one knee, holding a ring box out to me, with a smile on his face.

"I said that part of the game hasn't happened yet, J. But I was hoping we could write it together. I love you more than I ever thought possible. I know our relationship has been a bit of a whirlwind, but you once said that when your soul finds its tether that too fast doesn't exist. I've known you were my soul's tether since the day we met. So, I'm asking you, Janelle Lashaun Cross. Will you marry me?"

Sometimes, I think about the fact that I almost let Rome walk away from me. What would my life have been if I had only given him that one week? Then moments like this remind me that I'll never have to know.

I drop to my knees in front of him and take his face in mine. "You are the one person I trust the most with my yes's. So, of course, I'll give you this one too."

The End

Want more Janelle and Rome? Head to my website for a bonus chapter!
www.natashabishopwrites.com

ACKNOWLEDGEMENTS

To Janil—My bestie & sister, your support means the world to me. Without our writing sprints and checking in on each other I don't know if these two would've gotten their story. I'm still pissed about the fruit stand! I love you down and I'm so proud of how far you've come and how far you've yet to go. I'm so grateful for our friendship.

To Amanda—You are a raggedy heaux and all you do is bully me, hate on me, and convince your readers that I'm the mean one… and I couldn't love you more for it. Lmao keep being the heaux you are and don't think you can get rid of me because you can't.

To my soul sister—Y'all can thank her for picking the song that went with chapter four, she wants her credit. Thank you for all your support, soul sister. From roasting men, to you understanding why I needed to be a terrible mod, to our Love Is Blind think pieces, you kept me going through this book!

To Dee—We have become fast friends all thanks to the crack you put in your books. I've come to know I can count on you to be in my corner, and you can count on me to do the same for you. I'd bust my guns Nev style for you boo. Thank you for your friendship!

To my **author** friend, Miyeko—I am so proud of you and I can't wait to see your author career blossom. Thank you for always being a friend.

To Kim & Chula—I am so thankful for y'all every day. Y'all are badasses and I admire the hell out of you.

To Black AF Book Club—My forever familyyyyyyy. I love y'all so much. You hold me down through good days and sad girl days and it is appreciated. We gon be sharing islands, cells, and first class seats to hell for life.

To my Vulnerability Drive Babes—Y'all are all dope as hell and I'm honored to share space with you. I'm cheering you all on.

To You—The readers—Thank you all so much for giving my books a chance and sharing that love with me. It will never get old. Without you, this dream wouldn't be possible.

ALSO BY
NATASHA BISHOP

ABOUT THE AUTHOR

Natasha is an indie contemporary romance author living in Baltimore, MD with her family and fur baby.

She likes to write about everyday heroes who are a bit haunted and heroines who are sweet but also badass.

When she's not writing, she's usually reading, playing with her adorable dog, or hunting down delicious gluten free snacks.

STAY CONNECTED!

Newsletter Sign Up (https://geni.us/NBNewsletterSignUp)

Goodreads (https://geni.us/GoodreadsNatashaBishop)

Instagram (Natasha Bishop (@natashabishopwrites))

Tik Tok (@natashabishopwrites)

Facebook Reader Group (https://geni.us/NatashaBishopsBishes)

Facebook Author Page (https://geni.us/NBAuthorPage)

Amazon (https://geni.us/NBAmazonAuthorPage)

Linktr.ee (https://linktr.ee/NatashaBishop)

Website (www.natashabishopwrites.com)